Faraway Summer

Johanna Hurwitz

Faraway Summer

MCS
MENUCHA
CLASSROOM
SOLUTIONS

Menucha Publishers, Inc.
Text copyright © 1998, 2019 by Johanna Hurwitz
Typeset and designed by Rivkah Lewis
All rights reserved

ISBN 978-1-61465-762-0
Library of Congress Control Number: 201994500

Published and distributed by:
Menucha Classroom Solutions
An imprint of Menucha Publishers, Inc.
1235 38th Street
Brooklyn, NY 11218
Tel/Fax: 718-232-0856
www.menuchapublishers.com
sales@menuchapublishers.com

An earlier version of this book was published
by HarperCollins Publishers.
Woodcut image on cover by Mary Azarian.
Snowflake photograph on page 151 courtesy
of the Jericho Historical Society.

Printed in China

For Alice Bayles,

Judy and Joe Davison,

Gale Griffin,

and all my other

Vermont friends,

north, south, east, and west

JULY 31, 1910

My valise is almost packed. Tomorrow I'm leaving for two weeks to a place called Jericho. It's in the northern part of the state of Vermont. I'll be staying on a farm owned by a Jewish family who is related to a friend of my sister Ruthi. I know life in Jericho will be very different from what I know here in New York City. If I were going to the biblical town with the same name, it could not seem farther away.

When Ruthi said that she had filled out an

application to the Fresh Air Fund for me, I thought she was joking. How could my sister do such a thing without asking me? I'm not an infant. I am twelve years old, almost thirteen! But ever since Mama died last year, Ruthi has acted as if there were sixteen years' difference in our ages and not just six.

"Oh, Dossi, it will be a wonderful experience," she insisted. "The fund was set up to send young people like you away from the city and the dirt and the crowds and the heat. It's wonderful that the fund was able to find a willing Jewish family where you could stay. I couldn't let you go to just anyone. There aren't that many Jews in that area, but not only did they get a volunteer family, they are also related to our acquaintance Meyer Reisman. In fact, Meyer wrote to them and urged them to get involved. Now you'll be able to go and have a fine time in the country breathing pure air and eating wholesome foods."

"Suppose I say no? I don't want to breathe

air in another place and live with strangers. I'm satisfied being right here," I told my sister.

"Dossi. Think how sick you were all winter long. You hardly ever stopped coughing. I was sure you were developing the same horrible consumption disease that took away Papa. I don't want to lose you," she said, hugging me tightly. "You seem better now, but the country will make you stronger than ever. I'm sure you'll love it in Jericho. You'll have new experiences and make new friends. You may not even want to come home again."

I knew Ruthi was wrong about that. Truthfully, I was and still am very frightened of what is ahead of me. But once Ruthi has made up her mind, it's impossible to change it. "You said as soon as school was out for the summer you'd arrange for me to get a real job," I reminded my sister. I often help our landlady, Mrs. Aronson, take care of her children. That work doesn't put any money in our pockets. However, Mrs. Aronson says she charges us less rent than she would someone else because of my help.

"I never promised," Ruthi said. "Money is important, but we're managing with what I earn. You're too young and too smart to stay locked up inside a factory all day or sewing piecework at home. I want you to make good use of your time. Read books. Study. Perhaps your future can be brighter. Besides, you deserve a holiday from the Aronson children."

It's true that I love to read. I'm like Papa in that way. He was a real scholar and read many books before we came to America. Once we were here, he had to work too many hours, and his health got worse and worse. I have Papa's red hair and blue eyes, but I know I'm stronger than he was. Ruthi shouldn't worry about my health so much.

As soon as the letter came from the Fresh Air Fund saying that arrangements were made, Ruthi started going through my clothing. Even though she spends twelve hours a day sewing in a factory, she began mending and patching all my clothes.

It appeared for a few days this week that I might not go away after all. There has been a strike of the railway workers, and we thought there might not be any trains running. The strange thing is that I was relieved and disappointed at the same time. But today we learned it is the freight trains that have been most affected by the strikers, and although there are some delays, passenger trains are going through.

So now my clothing has been packed and ready for tomorrow. I've added a few little things to make me feel more at home when I arrive in Jericho. I put in the family portrait of Papa, Mama, Little Velvel, Ruthi, and me. It was taken when we still lived in Russia. I don't remember posing, but Ruthi says I was afraid of the man with the big black camera. The picture lacks color, but when I look at it, I can imagine Papa's red beard and the feel of

Mama's arm around my shoulder.

Papa went off to America soon after the picture was taken. It was three years before he earned enough money to send for the rest of us. By then, I had almost forgotten Papa, and Velvel was dead from scarlet fever.

Now both Papa and Mama are gone too, and there are only Ruthi and me and the photograph left. Ruth and Hadassah Rabinowitz. Ruthi and Dossi.

On Friday morning, in the midst of my packing, I wished I had a good book to read during my trip. So I left my things and went to the free lending library and borrowed two new books. My friend Mimi Sosnov came with me. How I wished she were coming with me to Jericho.

"Don't tell the librarian that I'm going to take these books to Vermont," I whispered to Mimi before we entered the library building. "Perhaps it is against the regulations. If I don't ask, she can't forbid me. And when I come back in two weeks, I'll return the books at once." The books will be three days late, but it will be worth sacrificing some penny candy to pay the library fine.

"This is a brand-new copy. You're the first person to borrow it," the librarian said, pointing to one of the books I had selected. It was *Anne of Green Gables* by L. M. Montgomery. I don't know if L. M. is a man or a woman, but the book looks interesting.

"Take especially good care of it," the librarian warned me.

"I always take good care of the books," I said, wondering if she guessed that the book was about to go on a long train ride with me.

"Let me see your hands," she demanded. "Are they clean?"

Luckily I had remembered to wash them before leaving for the library.

I took my books, and Mimi and I rushed out the door before the librarian could ask me any more questions. We giggled together all the way home at my close escape. "Let me see your hands!" Mimi kept repeating, imitating the librarian's tone of voice. Now the books are safely inside my valise.

I've also packed my autograph album from school with all the messages and signatures of my classmates. They'll keep me company among all the strangers I'll be meeting. And finally, when I finish writing tonight, I shall put in this new book of blank pages. Miss Blythe gave it to me as a prize for the achievement in our seventh grade class.

"You love to read other people's tales. Use this to write your own story," she had instructed me. And now I shall.

When Ruthi realized that I was going to pack my bottle of ink and my pen, she began to scold. "The ink will spill on all your clothing. You'll look terrible."

"I'd rather risk being covered with ink than leave it behind," I told her. But then I remembered the library books. "I'll close the bottle very tightly and then wrap it inside the under-garments that I've packed. That way, if it spills, no one will know about the blue stains but me."

Ruthi made a face, imagining me in inky underclothes, but she didn't say anything.

"Will you miss me?" I asked.

"Dossi, that's a foolish question."

"Yes, but you still haven't answered," I reminded her.

She stood for a moment looking at me. Then she began rubbing her eyes, which are always tired after her long hours of work. I realized all at once that there were tears in them. "I'll miss you. But I'll write and tell you about it."

"Don't spend all your money on postage stamps," she said, sniffing back her tears.

"You've given me fifty cents. That will be enough for many stamps, and candy and lemonade too."

"All right," she said. "Send me a card when you arrive so I know you made the journey safely."

"I'll find one with a beautiful picture," I promised.

So now I'm about to close my ink bottle and close this journal. The next time I write, I won't be on Essex Street. I'll be far away in the land of Jericho. Can you blame me if I am tingling inside with both excitement and fright?

August 1, 1910

Dear Ruthi,

I'm on the train and safe and well. The motion is pleasant and soothing and the views are unimaginable. They are like pages from my school geography text with so much green—trees, fields, and mountains. I looked from my window for hours until it grew too dark. I also read and admired the other passengers before I fell asleep. Sleeping while sitting up wasn't so bad. Still I'm glad we have a bed at home. I wish you could be here with me.

Your affectionate sister,

Dossi

The train stopped for twenty minutes when we reached Rutland, Vermont. Many people got off to stretch their legs and to buy food from the vendors along the tracks, who were selling fruit and sandwiches. There were a few railroad men with picket signs, but they didn't bother us.

Some people, like me, had to change trains. I took my valise and climbed down the steps of the train. It felt good to move about after sitting for so long. As I crossed the platform to my connecting train, I almost bought an apple. I had eaten the bread and cheese and all four of the bruised peaches that Ruthi had packed for me.

Then I saw a woman selling picture post-cards. When I noticed the colorful scenes of Vermont, I remembered my promise to Ruthi. I took my pennies and, instead of buying a piece of fruit, I selected a card for my sister. I couldn't find a picture of Jericho, but the one I bought was hand-tinted, showing a pictur-esque landscape: a lake surrounded by green trees. I bought a card with a different scene to send to Mimi, but I shall save it to post after I have been here a few days.

When I pasted the green penny stamp with Benjamin Franklin's face on the card for Ruthi, I envied it. I had bought the stamp at the post office near Essex Street before I left home. Soon it would journey back to the area from which it had come. My hours on the train were enough to feed my thoughts for weeks to come. I did not need more adventures than that.

I had a double seat to myself the entire ride. I was relieved that I didn't have to sit shoulder to shoulder with a stranger for so many hours. Still, I found myself as fascinated by the other passengers as I was by the views from the train window. Where was everyone going? It was interesting to make up stories about each one. I couldn't help wondering if any of them were making up a story about me, a twelve-year-old girl traveling alone.

A beautifully dressed older woman was traveling alone too. I thought she looked rather sad and guessed there had been a tragedy in her life. There were several men who smoked and read newspapers. One of the men snored so loudly when he fell asleep that I almost burst out laughing.

There was so much I wanted to tell Ruthi and Mimi, but there is too little room on a postcard even to begin. *Two weeks are not so long,* I reminded myself. Soon I would be going back home again, and I would tell them both every little detail about my trip.

The journey to Vermont went on and on and on. I thought it would never end. At the same time I knew that every moment I was getting closer to my destination, and I felt more and more nervous. I worried about the people with whom I was to stay. What kind of people would invite a stranger to move into their home and life for two weeks? Would they like me? And even more important, would I like them?

At last, the train pulled into the Jericho station. I picked up my valise and took a deep breath as I went down the train's steps. I looked about and saw a woman holding a paper with my name on it. I took a deep breath and walked over to her. She had a kind face and a warm smile.

"How do you do, Mrs. Reisman?" I said to her.

The woman shook her head. "I'm sorry, but I'm not Mrs. Reisman."

I blushed a bright red. Why was this other woman holding a sign with my name?

"Come. Sit with me," she said, pointing to a wooden bench. "Let me explain."

"I'm sorry," I told her. "But I have to watch for Mrs. Reisman. She'll be looking for me."

"No, no. She couldn't come," said the strange woman, grabbing my valise. "Mrs. Reisman has a sister who lives in New Hampshire. The sister was expecting a new baby in September. Yesterday, Mrs. Reisman got a letter from the sister's husband. His wife had given birth a month early and unexpectedly she had twins. It was wonderful news, but he couldn't manage on his own. He wrote begging his sister-in-law to come at once and help him with his wife and her two newborn babies.

"She didn't know what to do, and she had no way of reaching you or her cousin in New

York. So she came to me. We live just a short distance apart. She told me that she was expecting a visitor and asked if I could take over."

I looked at the woman with horror. She seemed pleasant enough, but she wasn't Jewish. The whole plan had been made because the Fresh Air Fund had a Jewish family to host me.

"I must go home to New York," I said in a quivering voice. It took all my efforts not to start crying.

"No, no. There is no train to New York now. And there isn't one tomorrow either. Mrs. Reisman said she had never met you. So it isn't as if you're missing an old friend. I'm Mrs. Meade, and I promise that my family and I will all take very good care of you." She pointed to a wagon nearby. "My husband and daughters are there," she said. "We all welcome you. My girls are close in age to you. I think you will have a good time together."

"What about food?" I asked. That was probably the rudest thing I could have said, but it just popped out of my mouth. "I'm Jewish and we have many rules about eating. I can't eat your food."

Mrs. Meade smiled at me. "Even though she had much packing and organizing to do, Mrs. Reisman sat with me and explained the full situation. I never hosted a Jewish person, but my family and I are all willing to learn. It will be a good experience for us all.

"See," said Mrs. Meade. "Mrs. Reisman even gave me a couple of dishes, a small pot and pan, and some silverware for you. No meat or meat product has ever touched them. This is going to be a challenge for me, but I am up to it. And it will be good for my daughters to see how other people live. My daughter Emma complains when I serve the same chicken dish two days in a row. I wonder how she would feel if she could eat no meat at all for two full weeks?"

I didn't know what to say or do. If only there was some sort of magic way for me to discuss this unexpected situation with Ruthi. This wasn't our plan at all. Even if the Fresh Air Fund had paid for my train ticket, they couldn't expect me to stay here.

"Come," said Mrs. Meade. "You must be very thirsty. I have a cool drink in the wagon. And there is nothing in it that is forbidden for you."

She was still holding my valise, but she put her other arm around my shoulder and led me to the wagon where Mr. Meade and their daughters were waiting. Even without having ever seen them before, I could tell they had on their best clothing to greet me.

I wished I were wearing something finer than my old skirt and blouse, but it was the best I own.

Emma Meade is fourteen, and Eleanor, who is called Nell, is almost nine years old. Both girls have long dark hair and they wear it in braids. "Your age fits right in the middle between my girls," said Mrs. Meade, smiling at me.

I tried hard to return her smile, but it was very difficult. It didn't seem to matter. Nell began to chatter away at once. She had a hundred things she wanted to ask me and another hundred to tell. She, and the others too, use some expressions that seem funny to me. I'm going to try to remember everything so I can record their exact words.

"Do you know Mary Wells?" Nell asked me almost at once.

I shook my head. The name meant nothing to me.

"I was sure you would. Mary Wells lives in New York City too. She was here and stayed with the Bentley family in July. She's gone home now," Nell explained.

"There are thousands and thousands of people in New York," Emma told her sister in an exasperated tone. "Of course Hadassah won't know Mary. It isn't like Jericho where we know everyone and everyone knows us."

"What kind of a name is Hadassah?" asked Mrs. Meade. "I've never heard it before. And I've never seen it on any of the stones in the graveyard either."

"I know two other Hadassahs in New York," I said, turning red. Those were the very first words that came out of my mouth speaking to the family as a whole. Ruthi would have wanted me to thank the Meades for inviting me to stay with them under these unexpected circumstances. She would have wanted me to say how happy I was to be there. But the truth was that I wasn't happy at all. I was miserable, and I didn't know how to get out of this situation.

"Hadassah must be a New York name," said Nell, taking my hand and squeezing it.

"It's in the Bible," I told her and the rest of the family. Mrs. Meade looked pleased when I said that.

I looked at the big animal attached to the wagon. "Does this horse belong to your family?" I asked.

"Oh, yes. This is Dandy," said Nell, reaching out to pat the horse on his rear. "We have one horse and six cows and a hog, fifteen chickens, and two barn cats," she announced proudly.

"Also one girl who can't stop talking," said Emma grumpily.

I couldn't resist smiling at her, even though I found Nell to be quite charming.

"You'll see many horses and cows as we ride home," Mrs. Meade told me. "Have you ever seen a horse this close up before?"

"I see hundreds of horses in New York," I told her. "Even though there seem to be more and more automobiles every day of the week, most of the merchants still use horses to pull their wares. There's the iceman and the milkman and the old rags man and the man who sells vegetables."

Nell sat on one side of me, and Emma sat on the other. "You must be very thirsty," said Mrs. Meade. She held out a large jar filled with liquid and poured some into a mug. "I put chips of ice in here, but they've all melted by now. Still, it's wet."

I was very thirsty, so I took a little sip from the mug. It had a sour-sweet taste that was not unpleasant and felt good going down my throat.

"Now me," said Nell, grabbing at the jar. The family passed the jar around with everyone taking a turn. I was the only one drinking from the mug.

"Switchel is good on a hot day," said Mrs. Meade when she took the jar. I guessed that was what we were drinking.

"Is that a kind of fruit?" I asked. "A switchel?"

Nell and Emma both began laughing. I blushed. What had I said that was so funny?

"Switchel is made out of cider vinegar and

molasses and water and a bit of powdered ginger," said Mr. Meade, grinning at me. Those were the first words I had heard him speak.

"Cider vinegar comes from apples," said Nell. "Maybe we should call apples switchels from now on."

As we rode along, Nell kept busy explaining things to me. There are two more members of the family, sons aged eighteen and sixteen: Edward and Timothy. "They are back home working in the fields," Nell explained. "And the cows need to be milked on time too."

"Nell, you're as noisy as a woodpecker," Emma complained as we rode along.

Mrs. Meade interrupted. "Actually, I told the boys they could take the afternoon off and go fishing. If we're lucky, we'll have some fresh trout for supper. Dossi should be able to eat that without any problem."

"Me too," said Emma.

It was the first positive words I had heard from her.

I didn't enjoy the wagon ride very much. In addition to my nervousness about staying with this family, my insides felt as if they were jumping about. Unlike the smooth motion of the train, we were bounced about in our seats so much that I worried I might fall out. The Vermont roads aren't paved the way streets are in New York. On one big bounce I accidentally bit my tongue. It hurt.

A fine dust was stirred up too as we drove along, and it got into my eyes and nose. Before long my eyes were tearing, and I started to cough as well. *What would Ruthi have to say about fresh air now?* I wondered.

Still, I had to marvel at the enormous fields of dark green that we passed. I'd never seen or imagined anything like them before. Rows and rows and rows of plants bending with the wind.

"That's corn," said Nell when she saw me staring.

"It's enough corn to feed all of New York

City," I observed with wonder.

"Not quite," Mr. Meade called over his shoulder to me. He's a very quiet man with a huge moustache.

"The corn is just about ready for picking," said his wife. "You'll get to eat a fair share before you leave here. We can roast it outdoors in the fire pit. No need to worry about my pots and pans," she added, smiling at me.

We passed many fields full of cows. I saw horses and sheep as well.

"The cows are lying down. That means it's going to rain," Nell explained to me.

"Really?" I asked. "Maybe they're just tired."

"Cows don't get tired," said Emma.

The sun was shining, so I couldn't believe that the cows knew much about weather. I thought they were just tired.

The houses along the way looked as if they had come out of my storybooks. Most were painted white and looked so clean. There were stretches of land between houses, not like in New York, where we live on top of one another. It was all so different from home. Yet at the same time I saw clothing flapping on wash lines, just like back on Essex Street. *Even in Vermont people have laundry*, I thought.

Another thing I noticed were the stone walls dividing the land.

"Each of those big stones was unearthed by farmers plowing the fields around here," Mrs. Meade explained when I commented on them. She pointed out how they were balanced on one another. "There's no mortar holding them together. There's an art to making a solid stone wall," she said.

"My brother Timothy can make them real good," Nell told me. "My father taught him how to do it."

Finally we reached the Meades' home. It is huge. Everyone in our tenement could live in it and there would still be room for all the other people up and down our street.

Emma and Nell share a bedroom at the top of the house. Next to it is a small room filled with trunks and boxes with still another bed, in the corner, for me. Imagine, there is a room just for eating meals. It has a long table and many chairs. With all that space, it was no wonder that the Meade family were so quick to invite me into their house. Wouldn't they be amazed to know that Ruthi and I cook and eat our meals and even sleep in the same single room?

In the kitchen I washed my hands and face. I had to work a little pump in the sink to make the water flow. If you move it up and down, the water comes out. Mrs. Meade told me that water is from their own well. I smoothed back my hair and hoped my appearance wouldn't have shamed Ruthi if she had been there to see me. Then I was ready to join the family around the dinner table.

I looked around the table at Edward and Timothy, the Meade brothers. They are both big, far bigger than any young men I've seen in New York. Their faces are burned brown from the sun, which makes their teeth look very white when they smile.

"We have our guest, Hadassah, to thank for our afternoon of fishing," said Timothy as their father portioned out a whole fish on each person's plate. My fish was on the plate that Mrs. Reisman had given to Mrs. Meade especially for me. The fish had been roasted over an outdoor fire and it sat on the plate with a potato that had kept it company while it cooked. There were also slices of bright red tomato. They were the most beautiful tomatoes I had ever seen.

"Let me help you," offered Mrs. Meade, leaning over toward my plate. She took my fork and removed the charred skin from my fish. Then she lifted the top layer of fish and removed the bony spine. "Eat slowly," she suggested to me. "There may still be some small bones within the fish and I don't want you to choke."

I didn't need her warning. I wasn't the least bit hungry, so of course I planned to eat slowly. But I confess that the fish was delicious. Even the baked potato tasted excellent. I suddenly had an appetite.

"This is so good," I said, smiling at Mrs. Meade.

"I'm glad you like it," she responded, beaming at me.

"Mother is an excellent cook," said Mr. Meade proudly, referring to his wife.

"Today I did nothing," Mrs. Meade pointed out. "Eddie and Tim were successful in catching the trout, and the fire did the rest. Good ingredients don't need much help," she said modestly.

"Papa planted the potatoes and I helped dig them up," Nell boasted.

I nodded. "I could taste that you had dug them up," I said.

"Really? Could you tell that I did it?" Nell asked.

"Of course not," said Emma. "Hadassah is being polite."

Nell looked so disappointed that I had to say something more. "These are the very best potatoes I have ever eaten," I insisted.

"The potatoes are probably fresher than any you get in New York," said Mrs. Meade. "It's too bad that you can't put any of my freshly churned butter on your potato, though."

"I don't need butter," I said. I felt I had to explain a bit to the family, so I added, "Jewish people like me are very cautious about what they eat and how they eat it. That's why Mrs. Reisman gave you special dishes for me to use."

"Don't apologize for what you eat and don't eat. I promise you won't starve while you stay at our house, and you won't break any rules of your religion either. Jewish or Christian, the world is big enough for all kinds of people," Mrs. Meade said firmly.

"Mary Wells came from New York and

stayed with a family last month. She ate everything. She ate lots of everything," said Nell. "I saw her eat three slices of pie at the neighborhood supper."

"Just because Mary Wells and Hadassah both come from New York City doesn't mean that they're the same," said Emma. "We hardly know any Jewish people around here in Jericho except for the Reismans."

"There are more Jewish families in Burlington," Mrs. Meade told me. "I even bought our sleigh blanket at a shop owned by a Jewish merchant there."

I looked over at Emma. She was looking at me suspiciously, as if I had suddenly taken on a new appearance since we had first met when I entered the family wagon.

"Does being Jewish mean you aren't a Christian?" she asked.

It seemed like a very ridiculous question to me. I nodded.

"We read about the Jewish people in Sunday

School," said Timothy. "The Bible is filled with stories about them. Sometimes they're called Israelites and sometimes they're called Hebrews. Don't you remember reading about Moses and Solomon and King David? They were all Jewish, just like Hadassah."

"Are you a princess?" Nell asked excitedly.

"A princess?"

"Well, if you're related to King David, you must be a princess."

Everyone laughed at Nell.

"No, I'm not a princess. I'm just a plain girl from the Lower East Side of New York." I didn't add that we were so poor that almost all my clothing was castoffs from other people, that my sister worked long hours to support us, that we lived in a single room in someone else's apartment, that the food on the table before me now was more than Ruthi and I consumed in a week.

"Thank goodness you're not a princess," said Mrs. Meade. "I wouldn't know how to treat you if you were, and we'd have to spend all our time making curtsies and kissing your hand."

"Please don't worry or fuss about me," I said to them all. "I'm sure I'll always find something here to eat until I go home."

"Oh, don't go home yet," said Emma.

Her words surprised me. Perhaps she was glad to have a guest staying at her house after all.

"Emma is right," said her mother. "It's an honor for us to host you. And we want you to have a good time here and breathe our good air and be exposed to our sun."

"Oh, Mama," said Edward. "Our sun is the same sun they have in New York City."

"I can't help being partial to our Vermont air and sun," said Mrs. Meade.

Mrs. Meade was not at all like Mama, yet there was something about her that reminded me of my mother. Mama could always say something to bring a smile to my lips. I guessed that if I had to stay in an unexpected house, I was lucky to have ended up right here.

We heard a rumble of thunder in the distance.

"Better check that the windows are closed," said Mr. Meade. "It sounds as if we're going to have some rain."

"I knew it!" shouted Nell with delight. "I told you that when the cows are lying down, it means it will rain."

"There are smart cows in Vermont," I said, and everyone laughed. I looked across at Emma. She is close to me in age and should be a friend, but she was busy stacking plates to take from the table and didn't look my way when I spoke.

It seems as if the Meade family is divided into two sorts of people: talkers and nontalkers. Mrs. Meade and Nell and Timothy are the talkers. Mr. Meade, Eddie, and Emma are the quiet ones.

I think I'll read some of the messages in my

autograph album. They'll remind me of the people who know and care about me back home. If I don't hear anything from Ruthi, I may have to stay here until my two full weeks are over. The train ticket that the Fresh Air Fund sent me is marked for my return on August 15. I don't even know if it can be exchanged for an earlier date. I shall have to stay here just one day at a time. That's what Mama would have said. And the good news is that I've made it through the first evening. Only thirteen more days until I'll be back on the train and going home to Essex Street again.

From My Autograph Album

Best wishes to one of my brightest students for a very bright future ahead.

Your teacher, Cynthia Blythe

———————◦◦◦———————

It only takes a little spot to write the words, Forget-me-not.

Your friend, Mimi Sosnov

———————◦◦◦———————

I wish you every possible happiness.
Your loving sister, Ruthi

———————◦◦◦———————

A few lines just for you:

————————————————

————————————————

————————————————

Your classmate, Annie Kazinski

AUGUST 2, 1910

I'd been rocked to sleep for so many hours on the train that I was sure I would have trouble sleeping last night. Also, I was afraid I'd feel lonely in the dark. I have never before had a bed all to myself. Even if I sometimes complain about Ruthi's bossiness and that she takes up too much room in our bed, still I am accustomed to the warmth of her body next to mine. It's a great comfort if I wake in the middle of the night from a bad dream to have her close.

They do not have gaslight here, as we do at home, so last night Mrs. Meade gave me a kerosene lamp and showed me how to use it. The rain had stopped, and there was some natural light too. I unpacked my clothing. The ink hadn't spilled! And I took out my books. I had read the whole of *Anne of Green Gables* during my train ride. It's a fine story. Imagine, Anne is an orphan with red hair, just like me. Even more of a coincidence, she goes off to stay with strangers. If only my time with the Meades could be as successful as Anne's time in Green Gables. I plan to read the book again on the way home.

The other book I borrowed from the library is *Little Women*. I've read it three times already. Louisa May Alcott is my favorite author. I've read all her books that the library owns. It's good to have Jo and Meg and Beth and Amy in the room here with me. Of course, I have the family portrait and my autograph album as well. It means I'm not alone after all.

I took out this journal and wrote about all that had happened since I got off the train. Then, at last, I changed into my nightgown and lay down on my bed. Its softness surprised me, for it was like nothing I'd ever felt before. At home Ruthi and I sleep on a thin, worn, sour-smelling mattress. Here the blanket and mattress both smell of flowers.

The next thing I knew, the sun was coming through the small attic window. I can't remember having ever wakened that way before. The cracked window in our room on Essex Street looks out onto the brick wall of the building next door. Ruthi doesn't clean the window for fear that it will break, so it gets darker and darker all the time. Even if the window was clean, we could never tell if the sun was shining or not. I looked out of the attic window and saw the Meades' cows grazing in the distance.

I didn't see anyone. I listened and didn't hear the sound of other people either. I decided that I must have wakened very early. Only the cows and I were awake! So I took my autograph album and reread each of the pages. I'm so glad to have it with me. I wonder if I'll feel close enough to the Meade family to ask them to sign my album when it's time for me to return home.

Now I think I hear voices in the distance. Could I have been wrong? Perhaps I didn't wake early. There are none of the sounds that I'm accustomed to at home to give me a clue. There are no shouts from the iceman or the vegetable seller. No loud cries of the Aronson baby in the next room. No squabbling shouts from the other children. They are always making a racket. Perhaps it's very late.

I think I must close my ink bottle and go downstairs. But I confess I'm afraid. It will be rude if I'm early and it will be rude if I'm late. But what can I do? I can't spend my whole day writing here in this room. Besides, my stomach is rumbling. I feel hungry.

When I went downstairs, I discovered I was both early and late. It was late if I was a farm-hand and had to milk the cows. Both Eddie and Timothy had done their morning chores and were finished with breakfast. Emma and Nell were still asleep.

Mrs. Meade was busy in the corner. She waved a floury hand at me and went to the sink to rinse both hands. "Good morning, my dear," she said, smiling at me. "I have a lovely surprise for you." She pointed to the kitchen table, where I saw a loaf of fresh bread and a plate with half a dozen brown eggs.

"Mr. Reisman paid an early morning call here," she explained, "and he brought these things for you. His wife may have gone off with their two young children to help her sister, but his elderly mother is still at his farm looking after him. She made this fresh loaf of bread especially for you. Isn't it lovely, with the braid down the center?"

I nodded my head. I had never had some-one make a loaf of bread just for me. "You must all share it with me," I told her. "And I will have to go and thank her as well."

"She also sent these eggs and this jar of honey for you. I guess she doesn't want you to go hungry while you're here. But you'll have a hard time visiting with her. She doesn't speak any English. Just some foreign tongue that I can't make out at all."

I laughed. "I bet she's talking Yiddish," I told Mrs. Meade. "I used to speak Yiddish to my parents. But I've forgotten a lot since they died. Now I only talk English, but still I could remember how to say 'thank you.'"

"Let me boil you one of these eggs," offered Mrs. Meade. "I believe they were laid just this morning."

I watched as Mrs. Meade placed one of the brown eggs with some water in the small pot Mrs. Reisman had given her and placed it on the stove. Then she went over to the corner of the table where she had been working when I entered the room. I saw her break an egg against the side of a bowl and empty the contents inside. "Oh, heavens!" I gasped.

"What's wrong?" asked Mrs. Meade, alarmed at my tone.

I pointed inside the bowl. There were two bright yellow yolks staring up at us. They looked like a pair of golden eyes. "I never saw such a thing," I said. "What happened? Can you still use the egg?"

Mrs. Meade looked into the bowl for a moment and then began to laugh. She threw her arms around my neck. "You poor silly child," she said laughing. "Have you never seen a double-yolked egg before?"

I shook my head.

"Of course not," she said. "I forgot that a city child like you will not have seen a lot of things. If you're lucky, you may even see a triple-yolker before you return home."

Flushed with embarrassment, I sat down at the other side of the table, and, using the knife that Mrs. Reisman had left for me, I cut a slice off the loaf of bread that Mrs. Reisman had made for me. The knife, the dishes, the specially made bread, and the eggs all amazed me. Truly the Meades' neighbors were going out of their way to simplify my life. I spread some honey on the fresh bread. It was delicious!

"Mr. Reisman even brought you a pitcher of milk from one of his cows," said Mrs. Meade as she poured some into my special mug.

The milk was completely different from the watery liquid we called milk in New York.

I heard footsteps on the stairs. Emma and Nell had come for their breakfast too.

"Hadassah! Here you are!" shouted Nell when she saw me. "We were being so quiet when we got dressed because we didn't hear any sound from your room. I even listened at the door because Emma wouldn't let me knock and wake you."

"Please knock tomorrow," I said. I smiled at Emma, but she just stared at me and didn't return my smile.

The rest of the day passed with a hundred new sights, sounds, smells, and tastes. After breakfast Emma had to wash the glass chimneys and the lantern globes of the kerosene lamps. Nell's daily job is to search for newly laid eggs. So she grabbed a basket and my arm as well. She took me on a full tour of the entire farm.

Just outside the house is a protected area filled with the most enormous pile of wood. "What is this for?" I asked. "Is your father going to build something?"

"That's the wood we'll burn in the winter," said Nell.

"You mean you'll burn all that wood?" I asked.

"Oh yes," Nell informed me. "It was cut a year ago and seasoned. My father and brothers have to start cutting and splitting the wood for next year. Without it, we'd freeze in the cold weather. Mama needs the wood for cooking too. Sometimes she calls it gopher wood."

"Gopher? Isn't that a kind of animal?" I asked.

"Gopher wood means that we put one armful of wood into the stove and then we need to 'go for' another. It's Emma's and my job to keep the woodbox inside the house full at all times."

"We burn coal in New York," I told her.

"What does coal look like?" Nell wanted to know. I explained that it was like black rocks. She bent down and picked up a dark stone from the ground. "Like this?" she asked.

I told her that coal was made out of some organic matter that had hardened over thousands of years. Luckily we had studied about it at school, so I could explain it a bit.

"It sounds funny," said Nell. I didn't tell her that some of the things I was learning about Vermont sounded funny to me.

We passed a small wooden house that Nell said was the icehouse. When she opened the door for me to take a look, a draft of cool air came out. Inside were huge blocks of ice, which Nell told me her father and brothers had cut in the winter from the pond behind the mill. I could see some shelves where Mrs. Meade stored the milk and meat to keep them cold.

"Archie, the iceman, drives his cart down our street every morning and sells us ice," I told Nell. "When it's a hot day and he's in a good mood, he gives the little kids slivers of ice to suck on." I smiled, remembering Archie lifting the huge blocks of ice with his metal tongs.

Next we walked to a still smaller wooden house, which was the chicken coop. Nell showed me how to look for eggs. We found an even dozen and put them inside the basket. One of them was cracked.

"That one is no good," Nell said when I handed it to her. "Mama will put it in the pig's mash."

"Why isn't it good?" I asked her. Ruthi always sends me to buy cracked eggs at the store.

"Dirt can get inside the crack," said Nell. "It could make you sick. Don't you know that?"

No, I didn't. And I decided I won't tell Ruthi either. Uncracked eggs cost twice as much as the cracked ones!

We stopped to look at the chickens. They were busy pecking at the ground and didn't pay any attention to us at all. The pig, on the other hand, came up to the fence of his pen and stuck his snout through the wooden slats so that Nell could scratch him. "Now you can see why I would never want to eat him when he's full grown," said Nell. "He's so sweet."

I would never think to describe the Meades' pig as "sweet."

We looked in the barns, where I saw two

cats but not Dandy, the horse, or any of the cows. "They're out in the pasture," Nell told me when I asked about them.

"Does your family own all this land?" I asked, awed by all I saw around me.

"We don't really have a big farm at all," Nell said. "We only have fifty-two acres. That's very small."

I've studied about acres at school, but I couldn't figure out the arithmetic in my head. All I know is that as far as I could see, the land belonged to the Meade family.

When we returned to the house, Mrs. Meade told Emma and Nell to weed the vegetable garden.

"Can I help too?" I asked.

"You'll be about as handy as a one-legged man in a kicking contest," Emma observed.

Mrs. Meade spoke up at once. "Emma, show Hadassah what the weeds look like," she said. "We don't want her to pull up all the carrot and tomato plants just because she's a city girl who doesn't know a weed from a window."

My face flushed and I felt awkward. It wasn't my fault that I didn't know what a weed looked like.

Mrs. Meade hugged me. "You'll be an expert by the time you leave us," she assured me.

"Do you want me to pick anything?" Emma asked.

"I want some carrots and beans for supper," said her mother. "Oh, and see if there's any rhubarb left. I'll make a pie for us if there is."

I watched as Emma pulled the orange carrots from the soil. It was like magic. She rubbed some of the dirt off with her hand before putting them in her basket. At school we learned about botany, but it isn't the same as watching an actual edible plant pulled from the ground.

Emma pointed out the weeds. To tell the truth, they looked just like the green tops of the growing vegetables to me. "Could you eat weeds?" I asked.

"Of course not. They'd taste dreadful, and they'd make you sick," said Emma, as if I were an idiot for even asking such a question. But I had a feeling she might be wrong about the weeds. After all, I eat cracked eggs and don't come to any harm.

"What's that?" I asked as she pulled up some reddish-green stalks that resembled celery.

"Rhubarb," she responded.

"I've never seen that before," I said.

Emma broke a piece off and cleaned it on her skirt. "Taste it," she said.

I took a bite of the strange vegetable and chewed it. At once my eyes began to tear from the sour taste and I felt myself gagging. I could not possibly bring myself to swallow it, and I spit the rhubarb out into my hand. How could the Meade family eat such an awful plant?

Nell laughed aloud. "Oh, Emma. That was mean," she said, but she seemed delighted by the trick her sister had played on me. "No one eats raw rhubarb. We cook it with lots of sugar and then it tastes wonderful."

I threw the half-chewed rhubarb I was holding onto the ground and wiped my hand on the handkerchief in my skirt pocket.

"Why are you so nasty to me?" I asked Emma. I kept my eyes down on my handkerchief so she couldn't see the tears that had come to my eyes.

Emma backed away from me. When I finally looked at her, I saw that her face had turned red. "Sorry," she mumbled. "It was just a little joke. I thought it would be funny."

"You better be careful," Nell warned her sister. "Hadassah will probably think of a joke of her own to get back at you."

"I don't want to get back at you," I said to both sisters. "I'm not like that. I can't help it if I'm ignorant about your plants. I bet there are lots of things I know about city life that you never heard of."

Emma shrugged her shoulders, but Nell said, "You could tell us about them. Maybe someday we'll visit a big city. So far I haven't even been to Burlington, but Mama says we'll go there one of these days. All right, Hadassah?" She took my hand and squeezed it.

I was still feeling annoyed with Emma, but I couldn't help liking Nell. She was so sweet. *It would be fun to have a younger sister like her,* I thought. "Why don't you call me Dossi?" I said to the sisters. "That's what everyone calls me at home."

"Dossi, Dossi," said Nell, trying it out. "I like that. It sounds friendlier than Hadassah."

I looked at Emma.

"But we're not friends yet," she said to her sister.

Now as I sit here writing, I keep thinking about Emma's manner. It is almost as if there was one of those Vermont stone walls separating us. I wonder if it will come down before it's time for me to return home. I wonder if we'll ever be friends.

AUGUST 3, 1910

Last night it was so hot that I couldn't sleep. The bed that had seemed so comfortable the night before was now damp with my sweat. My nightdress stuck to me, and a mosquito kept buzzing by my head. At home we have a thousand roaches. I hate them, but at least they have the good sense to be silent.

Finally, after tossing one way and another, I got up and walked toward the open window. I hoped there would be a little breeze to cool me. It was dark, but not so dark that I couldn't find my way.

I rested my arms on the window ledge and looked out. I wondered if I was facing in the direction of New York City and Ruthi. I had gotten through my first full Vermont day, but now that it was night, I missed Ruthi so much. Perhaps if I concentrated very hard, she could hear my thoughts. Perhaps she would write and tell me to come home to her. It was a silly thought, but that's what was in my head at that moment.

Suddenly a spark of light flashed past my eyes. Then it was gone. I thought I must have imagined it, but at once there was another spark. My heart began to beat with fear. Could there be a fire? I didn't smell any smoke, but still, I thought I should warn someone. It would be awful if the house burned down with all the family inside just because I hadn't said a word.

I made my way in the dark to the doorway

and called out, "Emma, Nell." Then I called again, louder, "Emma. Nell. Wake up!"

A door opened, and a moment later a bit of light shone on the landing.

"What is it?" asked Emma. She was wearing a long white nightgown and holding a kerosene lamp.

"There's a fire," I said anxiously. "Come, I'll show you."

I grabbed her by the arm and pulled her toward my window. "Look at those sparks," I said, pointing out into the darkness, where more sparks than ever were now visible.

"Oh, Hadassah, you foolish girl," scolded Emma. "Those aren't sparks at all. They're fireflies."

"Fireflies?" I asked, puzzled. "Do they bring fire?"

"Haven't you seen a firefly before?" she asked in amazement. Nell had joined us, and she began to laugh.

"You don't have to be afraid of them," Nell

said. "They're just little bugs. And they're perfectly harmless. They don't even sting or bite like bees or mosquitoes."

I stared out the window at the bits of light.

"Come," said Nell. "I'll show you."

Silently I followed Emma and Nell down the stairs. Emma led the way with her lamp. Nell opened the door, and we walked outside.

The ground felt cool and damp on my bare feet. I stepped on something sharp and called out with the unexpected pain.

"Hush!" snapped Emma. "You don't want to wake the rest of the family, do you?"

Neither she nor Nell seemed to think it was strange for us to be walking outside with bare feet or in our nightgowns. But I thought it would be awful if the rest of the family saw me this way.

"It's wet," I said softly as we walked into the long grass at the side of the house. I lifted my nightgown to keep it dry.

"Do," Emma said.

"Do? What do you want me to do?" I didn't understand.

"Not *do*. It's *dew*," Emma explained. "It's the moisture that forms on the grass at night."

Nell rushed ahead and called out, "Here! I caught one. Come and see."

Emma held the lamp close so I could look inside the cup of her sister's hands. There was a small insect. Even as I peered at it, a glow shone forth between Nell's fingers.

"It's magic," I said as Nell opened her hands and let the insect fly free again.

"No. Just a bug," said Emma. "Next time you'll know what it is you're seeing."

I looked up and saw the sky was dotted with a thousand sparks of light. But those were lights that I could recognize. "I never saw so many stars in all my life," I told the sisters.

"This must be very different from your home in the city," Nell commented.

I nodded in the dark.

We stood together in silence, admiring the

points of light in the sky. Suddenly I sneezed.

"Oh, dear. You mustn't get a chill," said Nell. She hooked her arm in mine and steered me toward the house.

"Are you having a good time here?" she asked.

"Oh, yes," I said politely.

And suddenly I realized that for the past half hour I had not once thought about Ruthi or Essex Street, and I *had* been enjoying myself. It was nice of the Meade sisters to get out of bed in the night to show me those strange fireflies. In the dark Emma seemed to be having a good time too. She hadn't complained that I had wakened her. Maybe I imagined that she didn't like me. Maybe I would have a good time here after all, I thought hopefully as I climbed into bed.

Just before I fell asleep, I wondered if my feet were dirty. I knew that Ruthi would not have been pleased if I soiled the fresh bedclothes.

Now I am awake and dressed and waiting for Emma and Nell to knock on the door and tell me it's time to begin my next day here in Jericho.

CARTE POSTALE

CORRESPONDANCE

August 4, 1910

Dear Mimi,

You would be amazed at all the animals that are here—cows, chickens, horses, pigs, cats. Yesterday evening I saw a pair of wild deer run across the field and into the woods. Every day I seem to see or discover something new. I'm having fun, but it would be even more fun if you were here too.

I wonder who you are spending your time with while I'm away. Do you miss me?

Your friend

Dossi

AUGUST 4, 1910

Here are some of the things that happened yesterday. At breakfast Nell said to me, "Why did you bring all your *old* clothes for your visit here? Mary Wells wore a new dress or skirt almost every time we saw her."

I looked down at the skirt I was wearing. It was the same one I had arrived in and worn the day before. I have only one other skirt with me. They're all I own except for a heavy woolen one that once belonged to Ruthi. I didn't bring that because we decided it would be too hot for this time of year.

"You can't judge a man by his overcoat," said Mrs. Meade to her younger daughter in a sharp voice.

I'm not a man, and I wasn't wearing an overcoat, but I knew what she meant. Still, I was mortified by Nell's words, and my eyes filled with tears.

Mrs. Meade continued speaking. "Mary Wells was foolish to bring so much good clothing with her. You told me yourself that she got mud on her skirts and even tore one of them the day you all went to pick blueberries."

I blinked away my tears and smiled my thanks at Mrs. Meade for defending me. She must have guessed about my wardrobe. Everyone knows that the Fresh Air Fund is a charity for poor city children. Mary Wells probably borrowed clothing from everyone she knew, the way Ruthi borrowed a shawl from Mrs. Aronson and a necklace from Mrs. Lefkowitz the evening she went to the free concert at Cooper Union last winter.

Later in the morning Emma, Nell, and I walked together down the road to the post office and the general store on some errands for Mrs. Meade. I was pleased when Emma began to ask me questions.

"I'm getting used to the fact that you're not a Christian," she admitted to me. "It seemed so surprising at first. I guess we must seem strange to you too."

Her comment didn't really make me uncomfortable. It showed she had some interest in me. "You don't seem strange," I said. "You all seem very nice. I like your family very much."

"Are we the first Christians that you've met?" Emma asked.

"No," I replied. "In my school there are both Christian and non-Christian students. And all of my teachers are Christian."

"New York must be so different from our little town," Emma commented. "Tell us about New York City," she asked me shyly. "It's hard for us to imagine what it's like."

"I don't know where to begin," I admitted. "It's so unlike your world here. It even smells different. Here I can smell the cows and the earth and the flowers. At home the odors are less pleasant. We live so close together that we breathe in what our neighbors are cooking for supper." I paused a moment.

"But not all the smells are bad," I added, defending my home. "I love to walk along Delancey Street and sniff the barrels of sour pickles and the herrings that the vendors have lined up in front of their shops."

"I like pickles too," Nell said. "Mama makes them every year."

"Tell us more," Emma coaxed me.

"I often walk great distances," I told her. "Sometimes my friend Mimi comes with me. There is a huge park in the middle of the city. It has hundreds of trees and grass and flowers. There is even a lake. But it's several miles from where we live. If we take the tram, we have no money for a cold drink. So we always have to decide which we care about more, our feet or our thirst."

I smiled at the girls as I remembered one of our walks. "One day we walked from our house all the way to Forty-Second Street to see the grand new public library that is being built on the site of the reservoir there. That was a long walk too. More than three miles each way."

"We have a library here. It's housed in a room in Miss Peabody's home," Emma told me. "It's open two days a week for three hours each time."

That surprised me. I'm glad to know a way in which New York is superior to Jericho, Vermont. The library I go to is open six days a week and for many hours.

"I brought two books with me from the branch of the library near my home," I said. I told her the titles.

"I've already read *Little Women*," Emma said. "And I read some other books by Louisa May Alcott too. But I never heard of *Anne of Green Gables*."

"It's a very good story," I told her. "I was so involved in reading it on the train that I didn't even realize where I was. I looked up expecting to be in my room at home and was amazed to see so many strangers walking about."

"That's funny," said Nell.

"That's happened to me when I read a good book," Emma said. "I enter the world of the story I'm reading."

I thought of something. "Would you like to borrow *Anne of Green Gables* from me while I'm here?" I offered. "I'm sure you'll enjoy it too."

"Oh, yes," Emma said eagerly. I was delighted that I had found something that I could share with her.

We walked along quietly for a time. Nell

stopped and picked wildflowers along the dirt road.

"What are you doing that for? We have those same flowers growing on our property," Emma told her sister. But Nell just ignored Emma's comment and kept on picking.

After a bit Emma looked at me and spoke again. "Perhaps someday I'll go to New York City. Maybe I'll come and visit you," she said shyly.

"Me too," said Nell at once. "I want to see New York too."

I looked at them, horrified. I'd made a point of not describing my home to them. They had no idea about where I lived. It's not a big house with many rooms like theirs. Ruthi and I live in a single room in the Aronsons' apartment. Our meals are mostly cold—bread and cheese and cold meats that we buy and eat on the few plates we have. Sometimes in the winter Mrs. Aronson lets Ruthi make a pot of soup on her stove. Sometimes she offers us part of the meal she has prepared. We always pay for our share. What would Emma and Nell think of our life after all the space and riches they're accustomed to here?

"Perhaps," I said, and Emma immediately sensed my reluctance.

"That's not very generous of you," she said, sounding annoyed.

"That's all right, Dossi. I like it here," said Nell. She shrugged.

But I could see I had offended Emma and I had lost my chance to become her friend.

I also noticed that while Nell had taken to calling me Dossi, Emma had not. It seemed a sign that she didn't want to become close to me.

Luckily someone on a bicycle rode past at the crossroad ahead of us, and it was a distraction. At first I thought it was a boy. But as we drew closer I could see his moustache and make out that it was a grown man. He lifted an arm and tipped his cap. "Good morning, ladies," he said as he went by.

Nell giggled. "He always calls us ladies," she whispered.

"Who is he?" I asked.

"Mr. Bentley," said Emma. "He's one of our neighbors. But everyone calls him Snowflake Bentley because he's so crazy about snow."

"He takes photographs of snowflakes. Isn't that strange?" asked Nell. "I bet you never heard of anyone doing that."

"That's true," I said. "I didn't know you could even do such a thing."

"We think he's a little bit touched in the head," said Nell. "You should take pictures of people. Not snowflakes!"

"Hush, Nell, that's not polite," Emma said, correcting her sister.

"You said so yourself," Nell protested. "I heard you talking about him with Tim one day."

"Never mind," said Emma.

"Mr. Bentley lives with his brother and his brother's family. And all the children have names that begin with the letter *A*," Nell informed me. "There's Alric, Agnes, Arthur, Alice, Archie, Amy, Anna, and Alwyn. Isn't that amazing?"

I agreed. "It's funny, but you know that there are three children in your family with names starting with *E* — Edward, Emma, and Nell's real name is Eleanor. Suppose your parents had given Timothy an *E* name too?"

So all the rest of the way to the post office, we suggested names to one another that Mr. and Mrs. Meade could have given their younger son — Edgar, Edwin, Emmett, Edmund, Elliott, Elmer...

But the coolness and angry words that Emma had said to me were still there between us. I can't forget them, and I'm certain neither can she.

From My Autograph Album

Be not false, unkind, or cruel.
Banish evil words or strife.
Thus shall each day be a jewel.
Strung upon the thread of life.

Your friend, Nellie Kenyon

Remember me in friendship
Remember me in love
Remember me, dear Dossi
When we meet in Heaven above.

Your seatmate, Heller Miller

May your voyage through life
Be as happy and free
As the dancing waves
On the deep blue sea.

Your schoolmate, Edith Thorn

When you glance at this page
Don't get angry and frown
For it's written by one
Who wrote upside down.

Your classmate, Nadia Snyder

AUGUST 5, 1910

Whenever I feel a bit lonely or unhappy, I turn to the pages of my autograph album. Then I can imagine the faces of my schoolmates, and it makes me smile.

Unfortunately today this remedy doesn't seem to work. That's because, in addition to being unhappy, I'm feeling unwell. During the night, I had to run downstairs twice to use the privy. There's a chamber pot here in my room, but I couldn't bring myself to use it.

Mrs. Meade diagnosed my ailment at once.

"Our Vermont milk is too rich for your poor stomach," she said. "I should have thought to dilute the milk Mr. Reisman brought you with water. It's a wonder you didn't get sick the very first night."

I thought back and remembered the first couple of meals when I drank the milk that Mr. Reisman had delivered to the house for me. The milk at home seems as much water as milk. Mrs. Meade was right.

So here I am, lying in my bed. Emma brought me a plate with a slice of Mrs. Reisman's unbuttered bread and a cup of hot tea. I thanked her, but I have no appetite to eat anything. I did take a few sips of the tea, however.

"Could I borrow that book you brought?" she asked me. I nodded.

"I hope you like it," I said as she took the book from the top of the dresser where I had left it.

Then Nell came into the room with a few pretty flowers in a glass. She put them on the dresser and whispered to me. "It's boring without you."

I reached out my arms and gave her a hug. "You don't have to whisper," I told her. "I'm not dying."

However, a little later I had to run downstairs to the privy once more. I did feel as if I were dying for a few moments. But the relief is great afterward. And just now I don't feel so bad at all.

I hope I'm recovered by this evening. Nell came upstairs a second time to tell me that we have all been invited to go to the Bentleys' house after dinner. "He plays the piano, and we all sing," she informed me.

"Who plays the piano?" I asked.

"Mr. Bentley." Then she giggled and added, "Snowflake. He's the one you saw on the road the other day."

AUGUST 6, LATE EVENING

I'm so thankful that my stomach was no longer bothering me last night. At supper-time I was cautious and ate only a little bread and some farmer's cheese that Mrs. Reisman had sent over for me. I also had a cup of tea. As soon as the dishes were cleared from the table, all of us walked up the road to the Bentley house.

It's a large farmhouse, not unlike the Meade home.

I met all the Bentleys, including the many children with the initial *A*. The father of all these people is Mr. Charles Bentley, who is the brother of the man I saw riding the bicycle. Wilson Bentley, or Uncle Willie, as everyone calls him, is Mr. Charles Bentley's younger brother. The younger Mr. Bentley is quite short. In fact, I believe he is smaller than I am, despite the fact that I'm still growing and he's a grown man. From the back one would mistake him for a boy. Then, when he turns around, you're surprised to see his big moustache.

It was the short Willie Bentley who made the gathering so much fun. He plays the piano.

Nell says he often invites the Meades over for a musical evening. Everyone sat about, singing merry tunes. It was delightful to see Eddie and Timothy joining in with the singing. Even silent Mr. Meade sang out with a fine deep voice.

Mr. Bentley played "Meet Me in St. Louis," "Daisy, Daisy," "Yankee Doodle," and many other songs that I learned at school. I enjoyed myself very much.

After the music Mrs. Charles Bentley served lemonade and slices of pound cake. They looked delicious, but I refrained from eating.

"Don't you like cake?" inquired Uncle Willie when he saw me passing up the refreshments.

"I love cake. But I'm not hungry this evening," I told him. I didn't wish to seem impolite, but it was easier than explaining why I didn't want to eat it.

"I hope you're enjoying your stay in Vermont," he said.

"It's a very beautiful place," I told him, "and the Meade family is very kind to take me in."

"We try to have one or two young people come and stay at our farm each year too," he said. "The Fresh Air Fund is a wonderful organization. If I were a millionaire, I would surely endow it."

"Emma told me that you've photographed snowflakes," I said. "I didn't know one could do such a thing."

"No one knew. Or at least no one bothered to try," Mr. Bentley replied. "But I've been doing it since I was a young man with my first camera. And do you know what I have discovered? No two snowflakes are ever alike."

"Really?" I thought back to the falling snow in New York City last winter and marveled at what he said. All that snow certainly appeared the same to me.

"Come over sometime during the day," he suggested. "I'll show you some of the pictures I've taken to prove what I've just said. You'll be amazed at the beauty and delicacy of the flakes."

"Oh, thank you," I said, delighted by his offer. "I would love to see them before I return to New York."

It was getting late, so we departed soon afterward. Mr. Meade carried a kerosene lantern to light our way, as it was now very dark.

"Hey, Red," Timothy called out to me. "Let me teach you a trick for walking in the dark. Put your whole foot down, instead of the usual way of walking, which is to place your heel on the ground, followed by your toe. That way your toe won't trip over a rock or fallen branch that you can't see."

I walked carefully, using Timothy's method. It must have worked, because I didn't stumble a single time in the dark. All around us were tiny sparks of light. Now I knew what they were and I could delight in their mysterious lighting. No kerosene lamps for them!

It's late now so I'll continue writing tomorrow morning. I hope I'll have an opportunity to see Mr. Bentley's photographs before I go back home.

AUGUST 7, 1910

Yesterday morning, Mrs. Meade offered to take me to meet Mrs. Reisman at her son's farm. It was near enough so we could walk.

The elder Mrs. Reisman was very warm and welcoming. I was right about her speaking Yiddish, and she was so happy when I could respond to her. She would have given me the entire contents of her kitchen if I had let her. I did take away a new loaf of bread and a strudel filled with cooked peaches.

Then she insisted we take a basket of

peaches because the Meades don't have any peaches growing on their land. "Tell her next time I will bring her some of our apples," said Mrs. Meade.

Mrs. Reisman said she had gotten a letter from her daughter-in-law. The new babies were doing well, but she felt she couldn't leave her sister yet. "She sends you a hundred kisses," said the elder Mrs. Reisman, bending to hug and kiss me. It was as if they had fallen out of the envelope with her letter.

That was the good part of the day. Later something very bad happened.

The morning, which had begun hot, had gotten hotter and hotter. So right after lunch, Mrs. Meade suggested that Emma, Nell, and I go to the pond. "I'll just watch," I said. "I can't swim on the Jewish Sabbath."

Emma and Nell put on their swimming costumes under their clothing. Emma carried an old quilt for us to lie on in the sun.

"I'm taking your book," Emma informed me. "I'm halfway through. It's a very good story. I really like it."

I was pleased she was enjoying the book. But at the same time I realized that, by taking the book to read, she wouldn't have to talk to me. And I never guessed that before the day was out I would regret that I'd ever let her borrow it.

As we walked, Nell and Emma taught me the names of the various wildflowers we passed. They're much more beautiful than the flowers planted in formal rows in Central Park. I learned to recognize Queen Anne's lace, black-eyed Susans, buttercups, devil's paintbrush, and goldenrod.

Emma and Nell splashed in the water. Then Emma got out of the pond and sat down on the quilt to dry off in the sun. Soon she was engrossed in my library book. Nell danced about, shaking herself like a dog caught in the rain.

I heard a faint rumble of thunder, but when

I asked if we should return to the house, both Emma and Nell assured me that it was far away. "Sometimes it will rain in Essex Center or in Underhill and we won't get even a single drop of water here," said Emma, looking up for a moment from the book.

I lay down on the blanket and felt the warm sun on my skin.

"Do you know any tongue twisters?" Nell asked me. She taught me a few that she knew.

A box of mixed biscuits, a mixed biscuit box.

Two toads totally tired tried to trot to Tedbury.

A swan swam over the sea; swan, swim; swan swam back again; well swum, swan.

It's a shame, Sam; these are the same, Sam. 'Tis all a sham, Sam, and a shame it is to sham so, Sam.

We repeated them many times and laughed at the way our tongues missed the words. After a bit, however, I became aware of a breeze cooling me. A dark cloud was approaching in the sky.

I was sure it would rain on us soon, but certainly Emma and Nell knew more about their weather than I did. So I held my tongue. Suddenly there was a crack of thunder that was much, much closer than before.

"Oh, dear," shouted Emma, jumping up. "Help me with the quilt," she yelled to her sister. They quickly folded it and grabbed their clothing.

It began to rain as we ran back to the farmhouse, shouting and laughing. Soon we were totally soaked! I had pinned my hair up before I went to the pond, but it had fallen down when I was running, and it was dripping down my back by the time we reached the house.

We rushed indoors, laughing and glad to be protected. As we dried ourselves, Mrs. Meade gave us milk with honey to drink.

"You didn't need the pond to cool you off

after all," she said to us. "And now that you're here, you can help me. I've begun canning our beans. You can trim the ends off them."

It was something I'd never seen before. We washed the freshly picked green beans. There were pounds and pounds of them. Then we cut the ends off, and Mrs. Meade dropped the beans into a pot of boiling water. She had another enormous pot on the stove with more boiling water. Into that she put the empty glass jars into which she later poured the beans. Then she fastened glass lids with metal wires that were attached to the jars. The jars were again placed in water and boiled to prevent spoilage.

The large kitchen became hot and steamy. It was tedious work, yet it was cozy to be working with the Meade women while the rain continued to pour down heavily outside. I wondered what Mr. Meade and Eddie and Timothy did in the rain. I didn't think they could work in the fields.

Afterward Mrs. Meade told Nell to show me the cupboards in the cellar where she stored her canned food. I was astounded. There were jars and jars of beans, corn, pickles, tomatoes, and spiced apples and strawberry preserves. The colors—green, yellow, and two shades of red—were revealed by the kerosene lamp in Nell's hand.

"This is what we eat all winter long," Nell said. "Every year we put up enough food to last for two years. That's in case one summer the crops fail and we can't put up anything."

"That's incredible," I said. "It's worth all the labor it takes." Then I noticed a row of tins. "What's inside those?" I asked.

"Maple syrup," Nell told me.

"I've read about it in a book. But I've never tasted any," I said.

"Never? What do you put on your pancakes in New York?" Nell wanted to know.

"I don't have pancakes," I said.

"Oh, how terrible," said Nell. "I'll tell

Mama to make you some before you go home. Everyone here loves them. You will too."

She led the way up the stairs, and I followed behind.

Emma and her mother were finished putting the canning pots away. The jars of green beans were lined up on the worktable to cool. Mrs. Meade went off to her bedroom to change to a fresh shirtwaist.

"Now I'm going to read until supper," said Emma. Suddenly a stricken look came across her face.

"What is it?" I asked her.

"I don't have the book," she said. "I left it by the pond."

"By the pond?" I asked, not believing what she had just said.

"Yes," said Emma quietly.

I felt sick. I had never seen a book that was left outside in a rainstorm, but I could imagine what it would look like. "How could you do that?" I whispered in horror. "You know it's not my book. I have to return it to the library as soon as I get home."

"I'll get it later when it stops raining," Emma promised.

"But it will look terrible," I cried out, my voice getting louder. "What am I going to do?"

"I don't know," said Emma. She grabbed my arm. "But if you're my friend, you won't dare tell my mother about this. And don't you be a tattletale either," she warned her sister.

"You don't care if I get into trouble, do you?" I said, full of anger. "You're awful!"

"You don't think *I'm* awful, do you?" asked Nell, pulling on my sleeve.

I shook my head, but I couldn't speak. I know that the librarian will never forgive me for mistreating her book. I have to buy a new copy. But where in the world will I ever get so much money?

Now it's Sunday morning, and all the Meades are at church. I was invited to join them. Mrs. Meade was very kind. She immediately added that she would understand if I wished to remain at home. I knew I could never go into their church. So I watched the whole family depart, pulled by Dandy, in their wagon. They all were dressed in their best clothes. Eddie and Timothy had their hair slicked back with water and wore white shirts and jackets.

Now I'm alone here (except for all the animals, of course). I've been thinking and thinking about the ruined library book. When Emma retrieved it yesterday evening from the ground near the pond, the pages were heavy with moisture and the cover was stained and swollen. "It will dry out," said Emma. Perhaps she's right, but it will never look the same. I know the librarian will be very annoyed with me when she sees the book. And I will have to replace it.

If Mrs. Meade had seen the book when Emma gave it to me, she would certainly have scolded her daughter. She probably would have made her pay for the new copy. But Emma was careful to give me the book when her mother wasn't about. And even though I'm furious at Emma, I can't bring myself to tell on her. I don't want to be a snitcher.

If only there was some way that I could confide in Mrs. Meade without letting her know that it was Emma's fault that the book was ruined. Perhaps she could think of a way to help me. Mrs. Meade has been so kind about everything and has been particularly concerned about my meals. I told her that I am very happy to eat the wonderful fresh vegetables and the homemade bread and butter that Mrs. Reisman sends me. But that doesn't satisfy her. She makes every effort to prepare dishes that I'll be able to eat.

Last night she served one of their own chickens, which Mr. Meade had slaughtered earlier in the day. She said it was called chicken fricassee and I could smell the thick rich gravy she had made for the meat. She knew I wouldn't touch it, but there was a piece of freshly caught fish just for me. I ate it with carrots and green beans and potatoes from the garden. It is amazing to be as self-sufficient as the Meades are.

A few days ago Mrs. Meade made a pie with the rhubarb that Emma had picked in the garden.

"It's delicious," Nell assured me. "You won't believe it's the same sour plant that you bit into before."

I didn't eat any of the pie because the crust was made with lard, which is pig fat. I shuddered imagining that! But Mrs. Meade had cooked a small portion of the sweetened rhubarb in my little pot for me to sample. I was amazed at how good it was.

"Poor Dossi can't eat a real piece of pie," said Nell sympathetically as she scraped the last crumbs of the pie from her plate.

"You don't have to worry about me," I reassured her and all the family. "I'm eating so much that soon my skirt won't want to button on me in the morning."

"Good," said Mrs. Meade. "I don't want you to return to New York looking as scrawny as when you arrived."

"Mama," Emma said. "That's not polite."

"Never mind," said her mother. "It's not polite, but it's true."

August 5, 1910

Dearest Sister,

I trust this letter finds you well. I miss you very much, but it pleases me to think of you in the fresh air of Vermont, even though our plans got so unexpectedly changed and you're staying with a Christian family. I was very surprised when I got your letter about Mrs. Reisman unexpectedly leaving town, but I'm glad she made arrangements for you to stay with the Meades, and even left you special dishes!

Here on Essex Street all continues as usual. The weather has been very hot since you left, so I'm happy to think that you do not have to suffer from the heat. Yesterday Mrs. Aronson told me she is expecting another child in January. This will bring the total number of little Aronsons up to five. She said that I needn't worry and that we can continue to rent our room because, after all, a baby doesn't take up much space. But remembering all the crying and commotion that went on when little Shlomo was born, I have some good news that I hope will make you as happy as it makes me.

Meyer Reisman has asked me to marry him! I am very happy and hope my news will please you as well. Soon we'll once again be part of a real family, and it will not be just the two of us alone.

I have learned a great deal about him since I first met him. Although he is only twenty-eight, Meyer is a widower. His wife died during a difficult childbirth four years ago. The infant died too. He was very unhappy and for a long time didn't think he would ever remarry. Then he met me! Because of the tragedy in his life, he has a compassion for and an understanding of our losses.

He understands that to marry me means that he gains not only a wife but a sister too. And that the sister will live with us. He insisted on that even before I told him that this would be a condition to my marriage. We both know that were it not for you and your cough, we might never have met—though I admit it seems strange to think of any illness with gratitude.

So it's to Meyer's three-room apartment on First Avenue that we'll move after I marry him next winter. It's strange, but I feel as if I've known him all my life. Remember that beautiful Sunday in March when it was my birthday? Meyer arrived carrying a bouquet of flowers and the strudel cake, which the three of us ate together. You could see then that he has both a warm manner and a hearty laugh.

In fact, I must now confess that it was Meyer who first told me about the Fresh Air Fund holidays. He suggested that I consider the benefits for you of a summer in a wholesome environment.

He said that he himself went on such holidays over several summers when he was your age. He stayed with a family in a rural community in upstate New York. (The father was a pharmacist, and it was he who encouraged Meyer to study in this area.) So now you see that your new brother-to-be has already had an influence on your life, and it is due to his urging that you are enjoying your current stay in Vermont.

Meyer says that after we marry, he wants me to give up my job at the shirt factory. "What about the money I earn?" I said. "I want Dossi to continue her education. Perhaps even to go to college."

"My new sister will have money for college," he promised me. To prove it, this evening he showed me a bankbook for an account that he has just opened in your name at the Bank of the Manhattan Company. He has deposited fifty dollars in it and promises to add more every year. That certainly proves that your brother-to-be is also generous.

I've never written such a long letter in my life. I could go on and on for many more pages telling you about Meyer. However, you'll be getting to know him very well soon enough. We'll both be at the train station to meet you when you return. In the meantime he joins me in saying he hopes you are having a fine visit. We will see you soon.

Your affectionate sister,
Ruthi

AUGUST 9, 1910

So much has happened since I last wrote. Last night I had trouble falling asleep. I couldn't lie still on the soft mattress. I turned and turned, thinking about so many things. First of all there was the letter that had come from Ruthi. Emma and Nell and I had walked to the post office to get Mr. Meade's weekly paper and whatever else the post might bring. Mrs. Meade was hoping for a letter from her aunt, who lives in Springfield, Massachusetts.

Instead there was a letter for me from *my* sister.

Nell wanted me to open it at once. "I've never received a letter," she said enviously.

"Neither have I," I admitted. Though I was very eager to read Ruthi's message, I wanted to read it in the privacy of my bedroom and not share it with anyone. So I put it in my pocket and waited impatiently till after lunch.

When I read Ruthi's words, I felt dizzy. Our whole life is about to change because my sister is going to get married! Who is this Meyer Reisman that he can upset our life so drastically? Of course I've met him a couple of times. But I don't really *know* him at all, only his outward appearance. He's short and beginning to lose his hair. I think when I get married, I'll want my husband to be more handsome. I can't imagine living with Meyer Reisman, and now I must share my sister with him.

And how dare he demand that Ruthi give

up her job at the factory? I can remember how delighted she was when she was hired there.

Ruthi says that Meyer is kind and generous and that I will grow to know him soon. I wonder if this is so. Do I need a brother? And isn't Ruthi too young to get married? It's true that our parents were married when Mama was just seventeen, a full year younger than Ruthi. Still, that was in Russia. Life was different there. The unexpectedness of Ruthi's news churns in my stomach just as the rich food did a few days ago. It will take some time until I can adjust to it all.

There's something else in Ruthi's letter for me to think about. She writes about my going to college. In June Miss Blythe told me that I must seriously consider continuing my education. She said I was too good a student to drop out of school the moment the law said I was old enough to do so. That got me thinking, and I told Ruthi that I would like to be a teacher instead of a factory worker. Now

I know that she has never forgotten those words of mine.

As if all this weren't enough, I had a more immediate problem to worry about as well — my library book. The pages are drying out. But it is no longer the perfect new book that I borrowed from the library.

"Oh, Hadassah, I'm so sorry," Emma said when we looked at it together yesterday. "You know I didn't do it on purpose."

"Of course I know that," I said sourly, "but that won't make a difference when I take the book into the library." As far as I'm concerned, every page of that book shows Emma's carelessness. I worry that I'll never be permitted to borrow another volume from the library. What an awful punishment that would be!

While I tossed in bed, troubled by all these different thoughts, it grew later and later. Suddenly I became aware of a smoky odor in the air. Was Mr. Meade standing in front of the house and smoking his pipe? I wondered.

I got out of bed and went to my window. The night was dark without a moon, and I couldn't see anyone below. I listened for footsteps. There was nothing. Then off in the distance I saw a flash of light. It must be one of those fireflies, I thought. Then I saw it again. It was not the golden light of the insect but a red glow. There was a real fire somewhere nearby.

Although the night was warm, I shivered with fear. I rushed to the door across the hall and knocked loudly. "Emma, Nell," I shouted.

Then I turned the knob and opened it. "There's a fire!" I called to the sleeping sisters inside the room. "Help me wake everyone."

I heard a match strike, and a moment later Emma had lit the kerosene lamp beside the bed.

"Hadassah Rabinowitz," she said harshly, "is that all you can do? Imagine fires every night?"

"No, no. This isn't like last time. This is a real fire. I'm certain of it."

"I smell smoke," said a sleepy voice. It was Nell.

Emma took a deep breath. "I think you're right," she conceded. "Quickly. We must rouse everyone."

Eddie and Timothy and the elder Meades all work very hard each day, so it is no wonder that they sleep deeply and had been unaware of the fire. But within moments the house was filled with light and commotion.

"Grab all the buckets," Mr. Meade called to his family as he tucked his nightshirt into his trousers. In a moment Eddie and Timothy rushed out to the barn and returned with the milk pails. I didn't know what they were for, but I carried a huge soup pot that Mrs. Meade thrust into my arms. And now that I know how to walk in the dark, I quickly followed the Meade family across the meadow.

The smell of smoke grew stronger and stronger as we walked.

"It's the Turners' barn," shouted Mr.

Meade. He had run way ahead of the rest of us in the direction of the fire. "Thank God their house is not attached to it!"

We all were out of breath as we approached. There were huge flames everywhere. I could hear the crackling sound of burning wood and the anguished voices of people and the cries of animals too. It was a horrible and frightening sight, and I began to tremble.

"Are the animals out?" shouted Mrs. Meade above the noises.

Mr. Meade disappeared inside the burning barn.

"Oh, no," shouted Nell, sobbing. "He'll be killed by the fire. I know it!"

"Shhh," Emma said, putting her arms around her sister and trying to comfort her. But by the light of the flames I could see the fear on her face too.

Then, miraculously, covered with soot, Mr. Meade came out of the barn, leading a horse that seemed wild with fear.

I saw other horses and cows being shooed to a far-off field. I wondered if any more animals were still inside the burning barn.

We were not the only people roused from our beds. Before long Mr. Reisman and the Bentley family were there too, as well as several other people I had not met before. By the light of the flames I quickly saw why I was carrying that big soup pot. We all joined the Turners, who, like us, were still wearing nightgowns and nightshirts. We stood in a line that went from the Turners' well to the barn. The soup pot and the milk pails, and all manner of other vessels, were filled with water and passed hand over hand toward the barn. By now the flames seemed to have encompassed the entire building. And even though I was many, many yards away, I could feel the heat of the fire as I stood passing each pail of water that was thrust into my hands. Smoke filled my lungs, and the crackling of the fire had a terrible sound.

It was useless. Even working as carefully as possible, as much water splashed out of each bucket as made it to the barn. I feared for the safety of Mr. Meade and his sons. They stood closest to the fire. Suppose some of the burning wooden beams fell on them! Somehow, in the midst of my concern about the Meade men and the Turner barn, my mind flew to Ruthi working on the top floor of the shirt factory. I have seen where she works. The windows are nailed shut. Suppose there was a fire while she was working inside. How could she get out? I don't know why I had that thought just then. But the possibility of my sister being in such a horrible danger made me shudder, and I lopped more water than ever onto myself and the ground.

"Watch what you're doing," a voice yelled at me.

I grabbed the next pail that came toward me and the next and the next.

Eventually, when we all were so exhausted

that I didn't think we could possibly pass another bucket, the fire was extinguished. But it was not because we had successfully doused it with the water. Rather, it had burned itself out. The barn was nothing more than a collection of blackened timbers, and the hay was totally consumed by the flames.

Mr. Meade and his sons remained behind with some of their other neighbors to soak the ground around the barn area. "They must watch that the fire doesn't start up elsewhere," Mrs. Meade explained to me as we walked back, wet, sooty, and worn out from our firefighting efforts. "Sometimes plant roots are on fire and the burning continues unseen underground. So the danger of fire won't be over until the next good rainstorm."

"How did the fire start?" I asked.

"Maybe someone knocked over a kerosene lamp," suggested Emma.

"There are many ways for a fire to begin," said Mrs. Meade. "A burning cigarette, a kerosene lamp, a bolt of lightning. One must always be on guard. Fire is a terrible disaster for a farmer."

"Fire is terrible for everyone," I said. "We have fires in New York City, but the fire department sends trucks loaded with water to help put them out. Our tenement has special iron steps so that people can climb downstairs and be rescued if there is a fire." Was there a fire escape at Ruthi's factory? I couldn't remember.

"There is a fire department here too," said Nell. "But they don't know when we have a fire so far from the center of town. Someday everyone will have telephones and be able to notify the firefighters. Then they could get here quickly. I heard Papa say it."

"Yes," said her mother. "And the sooner the better. You can't keep trouble from coming, but you don't have to give it a chair to sit in."

"I heard Mr. Turner say he was relieved that all his livestock was saved," said Emma consolingly.

"True. But his cows won't give milk anymore this summer," said Mrs. Meade. "A fright like this will dry them up."

"And poor Mr. Turner lost his barn," I added.

"They say it makes a difference whose cow is in the well," said Mrs. Meade, "but around here we all help one another rebuild after a disaster like this. It could happen to any of us anytime. We all know that. If we didn't help one another, we couldn't survive."

As we walked back toward the house, the sky was already getting light and birds were beginning to sing their morning songs. But I still kept thinking about the fire. The Meades were so rich compared with Ruthi and me. They had a big house, land, and plenty of food. But now I realized that they had plenty of worries too. If the weather wasn't good, their crops could fail. Sickness could attack them at any time, just as it attacked people in the city. If there was a fire, they could lose everything in an hour.

Suddenly the damaged library book seemed a very minor problem. No one's life was endangered by a soiled volume. I still knew that I had to resolve what I would do about it, but it no longer weighed on me so heavily.

I walked toward Emma and took her hand. "I forgive you for what happened to the library book," I said softly. "I'm sorry I was angry with you."

Emma looked at me and then squeezed my fingers. "Dossi," she said, "I've thought of a way that we can make money. Enough money to buy a new book."

My heart filled with happiness. But whether it was because Emma had a plan or because it was the first time she called me Dossi I cannot say.

CARTE POSTALE

CORRESPONDANCE

Dear Ruthie,

August 1, 1910

We are on the train and safe and well. The motion is pleasant and soothing and the sights are unimaginable. They are like pages from my school geography text with us moving through the green-green fields and mountains. I looked from my window for hours until it was too dark. I also read and admired the ...

... spending while eating ...

... you could be here with me.

Your affectionate sister,
Dossi

AUGUST 10, 1910

H ere is Emma's plan: We're going to pick wild blueberries and sell them to the general store. Emma says we can get ten cents a quart. If we both pick and Nell helps too, before long we'll earn enough money to pay for the ruined library book.

I'm eager to begin picking. Unfortunately it began to rain an hour after Emma revealed her plan. The rain was a blessing, according to Mrs. Meade. It meant that any smoldering plant roots near the Turner barn would certainly be extinguished.

"The rain's important for growing berries too," Emma said to console me.

But if it doesn't stop raining, we can't go picking. Wet berries quickly turn moldy, according to Emma.

Anyhow, since I couldn't pick berries, I decided this was a good day to visit Wilson Bentley. When I told Mrs. Meade that he'd invited me to see his photographs, she smiled and nodded. "I'll take you," she promised me.

"Uncle Willie is as proud as a dog with two tails with those pictures he's taken. They're amazing. We've all seen them about a hundred times already. The girls can cut up more vegetables for canning while we're away."

"Can't we go with you?" Nell begged.

"No. Stay here and do some work. You've seen the pictures before and you'll see them again," her mother said.

So Mrs. Meade and I went off in the rain. I

wore an old shawl of Mrs. Meade's over my head for protection. I was a bit shy of funny little Uncle Willie, so I was glad to have Mrs. Meade along for company. She's never at a loss for words. It was comforting to have her standing nearby when we arrived at the Bentley house.

As it turned out, however, quiet William Bentley becomes very excited when he starts talking about his snowflake photographs.

His blue eyes shone intently, and he lectured me with great passion about the marvels of nature. "Uncle Willie," I asked, "did you study about all this at college?"

"I never went to any classes beyond the local school," he said. "I'm sorry now. There is so much I'll never know, though I read and read what others have written."

"I think you must know as much as a college professor," I said, looking at picture after picture. Before me were the most amazing six-pointed images, each one delicate, each one just as beautiful as the one I'd admired a moment before. Perhaps strangest of all was the knowledge that I was looking at photographs of *snowflakes.*

"Notice that no two are the same," said Uncle Willie. "Though they exist side by side, each is different and unique. Just like human beings."

He was right. I'd never thought of it that way. But it's true. No two people are ever exactly alike, even two sisters like Ruthi and me or Emma and Nell.

I looked down at the snowflake photographs again. "These are all so beautiful," I said. "They should be in a book so everyone could see all these pictures."

"Perhaps someday that will come to pass. It's one of my dreams," Uncle Willie said hopefully. "In the meantime, however, I've written a few articles about what I've learned. I'm very pleased to know that my words have been published and can be read by people I'll never meet. Why, do you know the journals that printed my pieces are on file in big public and university libraries all over the country? Imagine that!"

"They're completing work on an enormous library in New York City," I told him, just as I had told Emma and Nell. "It's all made of marble, and it will be a research library for scholars and ordinary citizens to use. I'm sure your articles will be in there too."

"When the library opens, you must go and check," Uncle Willie told me. Then he said, "Do you know that your new library used to be in Vermont?"

"Used to be in Vermont?" I repeated.

"Yes indeed. Every piece of marble that was used to build that grand New York library came from the quarries here in Vermont. From Dorset, Vermont, to be exact. I read all about it in the newspaper."

"Really?" I asked. He nodded.

"What an amazing coincidence," I told him.

"It's funny to think that even before I ever set foot in Vermont, I'd seen a chunk of the state that had come to settle in New York City."

He smiled at my words. "Vermont is a beautiful place," he said. "Someday you must come visit us in the winter, when it's painted white with frost and snow. I feel very blessed to have had the good fortune of being born right here, in Jericho, in the very house where I still live. To me it is the most beautiful place on earth. Perhaps that's why I've never traveled very far from here. But sometimes I think I should have gone off to college."

"You could still go," I suggested.

"No," he said. "I'm not a young man anymore. There's too much work for me to do right here. There are thousands of pictures for me still to take. Not just snowflakes, but ice crystals and dewdrops too. Each tells us a story, don't you know?"

I nodded. It seemed funny to be standing in my damp clothing in the wooden shed, where

Uncle Willie does his work, and listening to him lecture to me and Mrs. Meade. But the words he said are still echoing in my head.

Before I left, he gave me a gift. "Pick one for yourself," he offered, pointing to the stack of photographs on the table.

It wasn't easy. Each snowflake seemed more beautiful than the one before.

"Sometimes in life one just has to act," said Uncle Willie when I seemed unable to make a decision.

"You're right," I agreed, and pointed to the snowflake closest at hand.

"It's yours!" he said. He took out his pen and signed his name and the date on the back of the photograph. Then he wrapped my picture in several sheets of old newspaper to protect it, even though the rain seemed to be letting up.

"Thank you," I said to the small man. "I'll never forget what you've shown and told me."

"And I'll never forget your kind interest," he said as I walked out the door.

It's easy to see why the townspeople call him Snowflake Bentley. But now that I've spoken with him at length, I realize that the name does not mock him but is given in love.

Soon it will be suppertime. Since the rain continued off and on all day, Mr. Meade and his sons went fishing. Mrs. Meade has prepared the trout they caught for our meal. Now, however, the rain seems to have really stopped.

If tomorrow is clear, Emma and Nell and I will begin picking berries. As I'm going home in just a few more days, we haven't much time to earn money. In the meantime I've put the damaged library book under the mattress of my bed. Perhaps the pressure of my body will flatten the pages and improve the appearance of the book, although I tend to doubt it.

AUGUST 11, 1910

Hurrah! The sun was shining when I woke this morning. Emma, Nell, and I ate breakfast quickly, and I helped them both perform their morning chores. As we rushed about, Mrs. Meade said, "Goodness, the three of you are as busy as butter on a hot griddle." She knew we were eager to earn some money, but she still didn't know why. Emma confessed to me that she has a reputation for being careless with things around the house. She didn't want her mother to learn of another example of that sort of behavior on her part.

Finally everything that needed doing was done and we could set off to pick blueberries. We walked up the hill to the edge of the Meade property. There are high bushes and a stand of trees. "Watch your step," Emma warned me. "It doesn't matter if you trip now, but you won't want to fall when you have a full basket."

The blueberries grow on prickly branches. I could feel the brambles through my long sleeves, but I didn't complain. Each berry brought us closer to our goal.

"Nell, stop eating!" Emma ordered when she saw what her sister was doing.

"We always eat when we pick," Nell protested.

"Not this year. In the past we were picking so Mama could make a pie. It didn't matter if the berries got inside our stomach straight from the bush or cooked in our dessert. These berries aren't meant for us to eat."

"Will Eddie and Timothy be disappointed not to have blueberry pie?" I asked.

"Mama can make an apple cobbler instead. The apples will be ripe any day, and that's their real favorite," Emma said.

The sun beat down on our heads, and my nose tickled from the scent of wildflowers. Bees buzzed nearby, and mosquitoes too. Sometimes I would see half a dozen berries growing close together. Other times I had to stand on my toes and stretch to reach just one tiny blue fruit. The berries were small, and it took a long time to fill a single quart.

After a while Nell grew tired and stopped picking. She lay on the grass watching us. I wanted to join her, but I knew I couldn't stop. Otherwise I'd never have enough berries to earn the money. Gradually the basket grew heavier on my arm.

"How much do we have now?" I asked. Emma examined the contents of my basket.

"If we're lucky, the berries that the three of

us have picked will fill three quarts."

"Three quarts?" I said. "That's only thirty cents. I need a dollar and a half to pay for the book. The price is printed right on the jacket. Do you think we're going to earn enough money this way?"

"Mama says to take care of the dimes and the dollars will take care of themselves," said Nell.

I hoped that Mrs. Meade was right about that.

"Let's take a rest," Emma suggested. It felt good to sit after standing for so long.

"I'll miss you when you return home," Emma said shyly.

"I'll miss you too," I responded at once, and I really meant it. These past couple of days, since the fire, I've felt truly at ease with the Meades. They've stopped treating me as a guest and more like part of the family. "You didn't like me very much at first, did you?" I asked Emma.

"That's because she didn't know how nice you are!" Nell exclaimed. "That's why she sometimes acted as cross as a bear with a sore head. But I liked you the moment you got off the train."

"Hush, Nell," said Emma with embarrassment. She blushed and looked down at the ground. "We never thought about having a Fresh Air visitor, even after Uncle Willie went about speaking to all the neighbors. He said we should invite a city child to have a good summer here in the country. But we wouldn't have thought to have you had it not been for Mrs. Reisman coming to our house. She was all flustered. She was looking forward to having you come and then suddenly it wasn't to be. She told Mama she didn't know what to do."

"And here I am," I said.

"You're so different from Mary Wells, who stayed with the Bentleys, that I didn't know what to make of you," Emma explained.

"Mary Wells giggled all the time. She told us fantastic tales about living in a mansion and having servants to take care of all her needs."

"Mary Wells sounds like a good storyteller," I said. "People who live in mansions and have servants don't need charity holidays in the country."

"I didn't think of that," said Emma. "Her stories were so good that we all liked to listen. She told us about the parties she went to and all the beautiful clothing and jewelry that she had at home. She said she'd gone riding in automobiles more times than she could remember. None of us has ever been in a motorcar."

Poor Mary, I thought. *Creating fantasies to impress her new friends.*

"I liked Mary Wells," said Emma. "Even though she held her nose whenever she went into the barn, she seemed funny, and she made me laugh. But now I like you better. You may not even be Christian, but somehow you seem just like us. You help with the chores, you're willing to learn new things, and you're honest."

"You helped save the Turners' animals!" Nell shouted out. "I heard Mr. Turner tell Papa that if he and Eddie and Timothy hadn't arrived when they did, he'd never have managed to get the horses and cows out of the barn. And Papa said, 'It's our city visitor you should be thanking. She woke us all.' "

I looked at Nell with amazement. I didn't know that Mr. Meade thought I was responsible for such a good deed.

"Do you remember when you asked if you could come and visit me in New York City?" I asked Emma.

She nodded her head.

"The reason I didn't agree at once is that we live so poorly compared with your family. But now my sister has written that she's going to get married. Soon we'll be living in a new tenement and have more space." I thought for a moment. Even *more space* in the city would seem congested to someone brought up in these wide-open spaces. Nevertheless, I went ahead. "Perhaps it will be possible for you to come after all. I should like it very much."

"It was wrong of me to ask you," said Emma. "Come," she said, standing up and brushing off her skirt. "Enough resting. Let's walk over to the spring and get a drink of water before we go back to picking."

I jumped up and took both of Emma's hands. "It's terrible that my library book got ruined, but it's fun to pick berries with you."

"I feel just awful about the book. I'm glad you've forgiven me for leaving it out in the rain. And I think this dilemma about replacing the book has taught me a better lesson than all the words that Mama has said on the subject. I know I won't act so carelessly in the future."

"I'm sure you won't," I assured Emma. "It was a good story, wasn't it?" I asked her. What with my concern about the book, we'd never talked about its contents.

"I loved it," Emma agreed. "Remember the part when Anne dyes her hair and it turns green?"

"Green?" shrieked Nell. "Green hair?"

"Yes," her sister told her. "She had beautiful red hair, just like Dossi, but she wanted to change the color."

We all laughed together at the thought of someone with green hair. And I was flattered that Emma had called my hair beautiful.

We continued picking berries until we heard the faint ring of the cowbell that Mrs. Meade uses to call her family back home. I was very hot and very tired, so I was glad that it was lunchtime. But it was a profitable morning.

AUGUST 12, 1910

That night Mrs. Meade made pancakes for supper. Of course, she made mine in my special pan from Mrs. Reisman, with the milk Mr. Reisman sent over for me. The maple syrup Mrs. Meade served the pancakes with was the most delicious thing I ever tasted. I'd read about maple syrup in our geography book at school, but it was the first time I ever tasted it.

"It's hard to believe that it pours out of the tree trunks in the spring," I marveled as I poured syrup on a second helping of pancakes.

"Not exactly pours out," Timothy corrected me. "The sap comes out, but there's still a tremendous amount of work before we have syrup like this."

The pancakes reminded me a little of the blintzes that Mrs. Aronson sometimes makes. Mama used to make blintzes too.

"Do you ever cook blintzes?" I asked Mrs. Meade.

"Blintzes?" Nell giggled. "What a funny word! Blintzes. Blintzes," she repeated.

Mrs. Meade shook her head. "What is it?" she wanted to know.

I explained that it's a very thin pancake onto which cheese or fruit is placed, and then it's rolled up. "If you added more milk and eggs to your batter, you could do the same thing here. And you have such delicious things to use as filling," I said, thinking of the jars of preserved fruit in the cellar and the fresh farmer's cheese that Mrs. Meade made from their own milk.

"Let's try it!" said Emma. "If it's good, we could bring blintzes to the next neighborhood supper."

Right away Nell began explaining to me that once a month the members of their church prepare a meal. Everyone brings a food item to share with the others. "Mama always brings a chicken potpie. It would be a big surprise to have something new and different to bring."

"I know many good recipes," I offered. "My mother made stuffed cabbage. I used to help her." It was funny how that memory suddenly returned to me. I had not thought about stuffed cabbage in a long, long time.

"Stuffed pancakes, stuffed cabbage," said Mrs. Meade, smiling. "You do have some unusual ideas."

"We have a hundred heads of cabbage out in the garden," said Timothy, "and there's a limit to the amount of slaw one family can consume happily."

"You're leaving in a few days," said Mrs. Meade, turning to me. "I guess you must begin giving me cooking lessons at once."

"Oh, no," I said. "You're such a good cook."

"Even a good cook, like a young dog, can learn some new tricks," said Mrs. Meade.

So this morning, before I went off berry picking with the girls, I showed Mrs. Meade how Mama used to boil the cabbage leaves to make them soft. Then she filled them with a mixture of chopped meat and onions.

After the "lesson," Emma, Nell, and I picked another two quarts of berries. I don't think there's another berry left in the whole area. And that's a good thing. I'm tired of all that picking. I don't want to see another berry bush!

All together we had about seven quarts. Seventy cents' worth, we thought. Not enough money for my needs, but it was a start.

Mr. Meade was going into town on some errands, so he hitched up Dandy to the wagon and drove us to the general store. I don't know how we would have been able to walk the distance, without spilling all our berries, if he hadn't given us the ride.

There was bad news at the store. Emma remembered that Mr. Clark sells berries each year. What she hadn't taken into account is that he buys them for less than the ten cents he sells them for. He offered us seven cents a quart. Seven times seven is only forty-nine.

"Oh, no," moaned Emma. "We need more money than that."

I didn't say a word. But I felt terrible. Forty-nine cents was less than a third of the amount of money I needed. "Tell you what," said Mr. Clark, looking at Emma's and Nell's and my disappointed faces. "I'll give you fifty cents. But not a penny more. And don't tell anyone about it. I can't afford to give my money away."

I swallowed hard and looked at Emma. She looked at me.

"Fifty cents is a lot of money," said Nell. For a moment she forgot we needed the money to buy a new book. "You could buy two pounds of candy or eight pounds of gingersnaps with that much money." She looked around the store at the different items and their prices. "You could get three pounds of English tea or two tins of talcum powder."

I think Nell must be a good arithmetic student, she was so quick to figure out all the purchases we could make. I looked at Emma, and despite my concern about the money, I began to smile. "Maybe if I brought the librarian some tea or some talcum powder, she would overlook the condition of the book."

"Eight pounds of gingersnaps would change anyone's opinion," Emma said. "It will also give them an upset stomach." She began to smile too.

Of course we didn't buy any of those items.

But we accepted Mr. Clark's offer and turned over our seven quarts of blueberries and received two worn quarters in exchange.

As we rode home, Emma said, "I have twenty cents in my handkerchief box. I will give it to you."

"I have five cents," said Nell. "You could have that."

"I still have twenty-five cents from my sister," I said. The rest of my money had been spent on lemon drops and licorice whips, which I bought for Emma and Nell and myself whenever we walked into town. I had planned to use the rest to buy a gift to take home to Ruthi.

"Why do you girls need money?" asked Mr. Meade, overhearing our comments.

"Dossi needs to replace her library book. It was ruined when I left it out in the rain," Emma admitted to her father.

"How much more money do you need?" Mr. Meade wanted to know.

"Fifty cents," said Nell. She *was* good in arithmetic.

Mr. Meade turned to me. "Don't worry about the money," he said. "Mr. Turner was asking me how he could reward you for rousing us the night of the fire. Now I know the answer."

I looked at him with surprise.

"Hurrah!" shouted Nell. "Now if we pick more berries, we can have a pie after all."

I rubbed together the two quarters that I was holding in my fist. The backs of both my hands were covered with scratches that I got while berry picking. But those scratches would soon be healed, and the book would be paid for.

"I'll help you pick," I promised Nell.

AUGUST 14, 1910

Yesterday it was the Sabbath. How quickly the days seem to fly by. I was very pleased when Mrs. Meade suggested that the two of us visit Mrs. Reisman again. "Until she learns more English, I must take advantage of you being able to speak for me," Mrs. Meade said.

Actually, we both wanted to say the same thing: a big thank you to Mrs. Reisman for supplying me with the new dishes and the kosher food.

Mrs. Reisman told us about the newborn

twins. At present they are so small that they sleep together in the same little cot. And sometimes they suck one another's thumbs for comfort. The image made all three of us laugh.

When we said goodbye, I gave Mrs. Reisman a big hug. It occurred to me that when Ruthi marries Meyer, I will be related to this lovely woman.

AUGUST 15, 1910

M y valise is almost packed. I woke early this morning, even before the sky grew light. This is my last morning here in Jericho, and in a few hours I'll be back aboard the train, going home. The train strike has been settled, so my ride to New York City should take less time than my trip here.

It's strange that I feel sad to be leaving when just two weeks ago I was so reluctant to come. But so much has happened in fourteen days. I've seen and done so many new things.

Yesterday I even milked a cow!

Several times while I've been visiting with the Meades, I've gone into the barn in the evening with Emma or Nell to watch the milking process. Finally, Mrs. Meade said, "Emma, show Dossi how to milk a cow. It's not such a mystery. Give her a hand if she needs help."

So off we went together. Of course, Nell came along too.

Timothy and Eddie had already begun the milking. It was fascinating to watch as they calmly squeezed the milk from the udders with the same ease with which I work the water pump in the Meade kitchen. If one of the cows swung her tail and hit them in the head, they merely laughed.

"You'd swing your tail too, if you had one," Timothy said when I commented on it. "In fact, I envy the cows. A tail would be very useful for shooing off the flies."

"Come over this way," Emma said to me. We walked toward one of the stalls where a cow was waiting. She pulled a stool for me to sit on and then she put a pail on the floor. I watched as she squatted down and showed me how to grab one of the cow's udders. "See. I just pull on one udder with my right hand and the other with my left. Gently but firmly."

As she spoke, the milk squirted down into the pail. When she did it, the task seemed so simple and easy. I looked at the white, foamy liquid. What magic!

"Old Bettie is the gentlest of our cows," she said. "Now you try. I know you can do it."

I reached out my hands and cautiously took hold of two udders. "Like this?" I asked.

"Pull harder," Emma said when nothing happened. "You won't hurt her. She's used to it."

I tried again and again. And then amazingly a bit of milk dripped down into the pail. "I did it," I gasped. "I really did."

More milk came out. In fact, it actually

squirted down into the pail.

All this time, Nell had been silently watching. Silence was not natural to her at all, and suddenly she didn't need to be quiet at all. "If you lived here all year, you could milk the cows every day!" she promised me.

So that was how I learned to do this amazing bit of farm work!

Supper was lovely. It was my last meal with the Meades, and Mrs. Meade had made it seem very festive. She had picked colorful wildflowers and put them in a vase on the table. And she used her best company dishes for serving the meal, even though I couldn't use them.

For a sweet at the end, Mrs. Meade served a delicious-looking golden brown cake.

"Do you know what this is?" she asked as she cut Mr. Meade a large slice.

"Cake?"

"This isn't just any cake. The recipe for this cake comes straight from the Bible," she said proudly.

"There're no cooking recipes in there," I said, wondering what sort of joke she was making.

"Yes indeed," she insisted, and everyone else agreed with her. Later, when the meal was over, she showed me a paper on which she had written down the cooking instructions. Each ingredient came straight from the Bible. I copied the recipe to show Ruthi. Maybe after she is Mrs. Reisman, she'll want to make this cake for Meyer.

Mrs. Meade gave me presents to take home. A tin of maple syrup and a jar of her strawberry preserves. I know Ruthi will enjoy them too.

"I wish I had something to give you in return," I said.

"But you have given us many things," said Mrs. Meade.

"No, I haven't."

"You certainly have! Your appreciation for all we have has made Emma and Nell more aware of their good fortune. And I for one am pleased to have finally gotten to really know a Hebrew person on such an intimate level. You may have some different customs, but deep down we're all the same. You're no different from us than our brown Jersey cows are from the Turners' black-and-white Holsteins."

"Mama," protested Emma, "you can't compare Dossi to a cow!"

"Mooo," I said, throwing my arms first around Mrs. Meade and then Emma and Nell in turn. What fine people they all are. Then I smiled at all the men in the Meade family.

Suddenly I realized that there was something I could give them. "Just a moment," I cried out, and ran up the stairs to my attic room. I took the copy of *Anne of Green Gables* from under my mattress. It still showed signs of the time it had spent out in the rain. But the pages were dry, and I could turn each of them. And the words and front illustration were there.

"I wish I had something new and beautiful to give you," I said, holding out the book. "But since I'm going to pay the library to buy a new copy, this one must belong to me. And so that means I can give it to you."

I handed the book to Emma.

"Oh, Dossi," she exclaimed. "This is a wonderful gift. And do you know what? Now I can finally finish reading the story."

"That book will remind you not to be so careless," said her mother, who had finally learned the truth about the poor book.

"No. It'll remind you of the fun we had picking berries," I corrected.

"I'll read it aloud to everyone during the winter," Emma promised. "You'll all laugh when you hear the story."

"We'll laugh, and we'll think of you," Nell promised me.

"For once our Nell is speaking some sense," said Mrs. Meade.

Now I think I hear Emma and Nell getting

dressed in their room. So I'll finish this page and close my ink bottle really tightly once more. I'll wrap it in my underclothes, just as I did when I packed to come here. The next time I write, I'll be back on Essex Street. I'm eager to see Ruthi again and to greet my new brother-to-be. But I know I'll miss the Meades and the town of Jericho.

Emma says that she hopes I can return next summer for another visit. That would be wonderful! Maybe I'll even meet the Jericho Mrs. Reisman then, and be able to thank her for arranging for me to stay at the Meades'. In the meantime, however, we've promised that we'll write letters to each other.

"Write one to me!" Nell pleaded. I remember that she said she's never received a letter. I'll be pleased to be the first to send one to her.

I know that I'll often turn back the pages of this diary and reread about all that happened to me during August 1910. And I'll

often look at the special pages in my autograph album where all my new friends have
inscribed their names. When school opens in
September, I must be sure to tell Miss Blythe
that I've filled so many pages in the book she
gave me. Won't she be amazed?

From My Autograph Album

You are always welcome in our home.
Sincerely, Ida Meade

Edward Meade, Sr.

Edward Meade, Jr.

Timothy Meade

Dear Dossi,
I will miss you. Come back to Jericho.
Nell

Dearest Dossi,

I will always remember you and the summer
of 1910. Please come back in 1911, 1912, 1913...
You have become my very special friend.

Your true friend, Emma Meade

May you be like the snowflakes that fall from heaven: discover your unique qualities.

The snowflakes melt and disappear. The memory of your visit will remain with all who crossed paths with you this summer.

Sincerely, Wilson Alwyn Bentley

August 14, 1910

BIBLICAL FRUIT CAKE

1 cup butter (Genesis, Chapter 18, Verse 8)

1 cup sugar (Psalms, Chapter 19, Verse 10)

4 whole eggs (Jeremiah, Chapter 17, Verse 11)

2 cups flour (Kings I, Chapter 4, Verse 22)

1½ cups raisins (Samuel I, Chapter 30, Verse 12)

1½ cups dates (Song of Songs, Chapter 7, Verse 7)

1 cup almonds (Numbers, Chapter 17, Verse 8)

½ cup water (Genesis, Chapter 24, Verse 17)

2 teaspoons honey (Exodus, Chapter 16, Verse 31)

1 teaspoon baking powder (Amos, Chapter 4, Verse 5)

pinch salt (Leviticus, Chapter 12, Verse 13)

cinnamon, ginger, and nutmeg, to taste

1. Take the first three ingredients and beat well.

2. Chop almonds and dates and add together with the other ingredients. Mix thoroughly. Pour batter into a floured and buttered tube pan with a removable bottom.

3. Bake at 350 degrees for 60 minutes. Test with a toothpick to be sure cake batter has fully

cooked. Cool in pan before removing.

4. This cake does not need frosting. However, if you sprinkle confectioner's sugar through a strainer, it will look as if snowflakes have fallen on the cake.

AUTHOR'S NOTE

This is a work of fiction. The Rabinowitz sisters and the Meade family exist only in my imagination. However, much of their story is based on fact. The Fresh Air Fund was established in 1877 and still exists. Its goal is to provide free two-week summer vacations in the country for disadvantaged city children. Well over a million young people have benefited from this program over the years.

I did not make up Wilson Alwyn Bentley. He lived in Jericho, Vermont, from 1865 to

1931. He did indeed photograph snowflakes and was the first to discover that no two flakes are the same. Essays of his were published in various journals, and in 1931, shortly before his death, a volume of his snowflake pictures was published by the American Meteorological Society. One of these photographs is reprinted in this book with the permission of the Jericho Historical Society.

During Bentley's lifetime, he was an active supporter of the Fresh Air Fund. Though he never married, he was close to his brother's family, made up of eight nieces and nephews, all of whom had names beginning with the letter *A*. He loved music and frequently entertained his family and neighbors by playing piano for them.

While researching information for this book, I read back issues of the *Brattleboro Reformer* and the *Rutland Herald* newspapers on microfilm. I traveled to Jericho, Vermont, and visited the Tenement Museum on New

York's Lower East Side. I listened to Evelyn Keefe, of Wilmington, Vermont, recount her memories of being a farmer's daughter in the early years of the twentieth century. The Brattleboro Museum and Art Center had an exhibit about farming in Vermont that I found helpful.

In addition, I read many books about this period and learned many interesting facts. Among them was my discovery that the elegant public library building at Forty-Second Street and Fifth Avenue, completed in 1911 and in which I was once employed, was constructed entirely from Vermont marble.

The Fresh Air Fund vacations did and continue to do more than merely give a holiday to city children. They introduce children from two different environments to one another, and this leads to growth and understanding for visitors and hosts alike.

ABOUT THE AUTHOR

Johanna Hurwitz is the award-winning author of more than six dozen books for young readers. Several of her books are about Elisa and her brother Russell. For many years Ms. Hurwitz worked as a children's librarian in both school and public libraries in New York City and Long Island. She lives in Great Neck, New York, and spends summers in Vermont. She has two grown children and three grandchildren.